CORGI in the CUPCAKES

Ben M. Baglio

Illustrations by Ann Baum

Cover illustration by
Mary Ann Lasher

SCHOLASTIC INC.

New York Toronto London Auckland Sydney
Mexico City New Delhi Hong Kong Buenos Aires

Special thanks to Andrea Abbott

ISBN-13: 978-0-439-02533-1
ISBN-10: 0-439-02533-8

12 11 10 9 8 7 6 5 4 3 2 1   8 9 10 11 12/0

Printed in the U.S.A.   40
First Scholastic printing, January 2008

One

"Science is just so complicated." Mandy Hope sighed, staring at the open book in front of her. Without taking her eyes off the page, she poured out some cereal. A slice of toast popped out of the toaster, and she sprang out of her chair and grabbed the toast before it could land on the floor.

Opposite her at the table, her dad, Dr. Adam Hope, shook his head. "That looks impossible to me!"

Mandy frowned as she sat down. "I said complicated, not impossible."

"Well, you just tried to do three things at the same

1

time: eating, catching, and reading," Adam Hope said with a grin.

Mandy laughed. "That's called juggling, Dad. And it's not what I meant. I was talking about physics," she said, pointing to the book. She was doing some last-minute studying for a test at school. "I've been trying to get it into my head all week, but it's so hard to figure out. And I know we'll get a question on it." She groaned. "I wish I could skip school today."

Her dad took a sip of coffee. "I remember having that feeling when I was in school. But you know you've got to do well in all the science subjects if you want to be accepted into veterinary college."

For as long as she could remember, Mandy had wanted to follow in her parents' footsteps and become a vet. "I guess so," she said, returning to the page in front of her. "It's just that I'm really worried I'll forget everything." She stared at a formula, then closed her eyes to see if she could remember it. A loud shout distracted her.

"Yikes!"

Mandy's eyes flew open. "That sounded like James!" She jumped up and ran to the window in time to see her best friend, James Hunter, skidding down the icy lane on his bike.

"Help!" he yelled, whizzing through the gate with the

wheels of his bike sliding out of control on the frozen ground. Strong gusts of wind made things worse, causing James and the bike to wobble. "No!" he shouted when a stray plastic bag blew into his face, covering his glasses like a blindfold.

Mandy flung open the window. "Watch out!" she shouted. Too late. The bike collided with a bush, crashed to the ground, and sent James flying. The plastic blindfold went flying, too, snatched away by the wind.

"Ouch!" cried James, landing at the foot of a gnarled rosebush.

When Mandy and her dad reached James, he was just sitting up. Mud speckled his face like freckles and clung to his jeans, his glasses were halfway down his nose, and a twig, caught in his hair, stuck out from the top of his head like an antenna.

"Are you OK?" Mandy asked, kneeling at his side. She expected him to groan in pain from a sprained wrist, a bruised knee, or even a broken ankle.

James looked up at her and grinned. "Isn't it just the best news?" he exclaimed, pushing his glasses back up his nose.

"What?" Mandy asked. James had to have a concussion. Crashing into thorny bushes wasn't her idea of good news.

"You don't know?" said James. Dr. Adam held out a hand to help him up, but James sprang easily to his feet and dusted the mud off the seat of his jeans.

"Don't know what?" Mandy asked, pulling the twig out of James's hair. As she did, she realized James wasn't in his uniform. And what was he doing here? He should have been on his way to the bus stop where she usually met him. It was clearly a bad idea to bike to school on a day like this. "We'll have to take the bus," she told him. "It's too icy to ride to school today."

"That's what I'm trying to tell you!" said James. "We're not going to school. It's closed."

Mandy stared at him in surprise. "How do you know?"

James picked up his bike. "The secretary called my mom to say the boiler's broken," he said, kicking mud off the pedals.

Dr. Adam winked at Mandy. "It looks like you'll miss that test after all."

James was inspecting his bike, checking the brakes and tires. Mandy saw that the front wheel was crooked. "Sorry about that," she said. "I didn't see you until you were going to crash."

James faced the bicycle and held the handlebars in his hands with the wheel between his knees. "It's not serious," he said, twisting the handlebars until the wheel was in line.

"Well, seeing as there are no broken bones or bikes, I think we can get on with the day's work," said Dr. Adam. "Maybe Mom and I can even count on having two extra pairs of hands to help us?"

Mandy's parents ran Animal Ark, the veterinary clinic that was attached to their home in the small Yorkshire village of Welford.

"You bet," said Mandy, who always welcomed any opportunity to help out with animals. She was already planning to check on an injured young fox that was being kept in the wildlife unit at the back of the clinic. She ran upstairs to change, and had just pulled on her jeans and a sweater when a car horn blared outside. "Now what?" She looked out of her bedroom window.

A pink van was coming through the gates. "Who's that?" Mandy wondered aloud as the horn sounded again. No one she knew drove a van the color of cotton candy. It stopped in front of the garage, and Mandy noticed a logo on the side — a giant red heart with a company name beneath it: CAROLE'S CAKES.

Maybe someone's sent us a cake for Valentine's Day, Mandy thought, running downstairs. Valentine's Day was just a few days away. "Someone named Carole just pulled up in a van that looks like a giant marshmallow," she said to James, who was in the kitchen checking the soccer scores in the newspaper.

"Marshmallow?" James echoed, his eyes lighting up. "Where?" He folded the newspaper and followed Mandy into the hall.

Opening the front door, Mandy was surprised to see Grandma Hope climbing out of the pink van. "Hi, Gran. That's not your new car, is it?" she said, going out to meet her.

"No, no. I got myself a cake route," Gran explained, straightening the bright pink sweatshirt she was wearing. "What do you think?" She turned around. On the back of the sweater was the Carole's Cakes logo.

"Um, very eye-catching!" said James.

"I didn't know you were looking for a job," Mandy said.

"It's not really a job," said Gran. "It's a favor for my friend Vera's niece — she's the *Carole* in *Carole's Cakes*." She pointed to the slogan on the van. "Carole's just starting her new business. I'm helping her by delivering the cakes around Welford for a few days."

"Cool job," commented James, peering through the back window.

Gran chuckled. "Sorry, no cakes in there yet, James. I took the van home last night to get used to driving it. But I'm on my way to pick up the orders from Carole now." She glanced at her watch. "Shouldn't you two be on your way to school?"

Mandy told her about the broken boiler.

"Well, seeing as you're free for the day, what about coming with me on my rounds this morning?" said Gran. "I could do with some extra pairs of hands."

James laughed. "That's what everyone's saying to us."

"Does that mean you're fully booked already?" said Gran.

"Not really," Mandy said. "We could go on the rounds with you this morning and help out here this afternoon."

After checking with her parents, Mandy and James squashed up next to Gran in the pink van and set off down the road, the little van bouncing over the potholes.

Carole lived a few miles away in a quaint stone cottage on the outskirts of Welford. "More willing workers," she said, chuckling as Gran introduced her to Mandy and James. She wore a flour-dusted apron decorated with strawberries and had curly auburn hair clipped back from her face. Her eyes were a deep blue, and her smile was warm and friendly. "Everything's ready," she said, taking them into the kitchen where the table was almost buried under bright pink cake boxes. On each of them was Carole's heart-shaped logo and telephone number.

"OK," said Gran. "We'll start packing these into the back of the van."

"Here's the delivery list," said Carole. Just then the phone rang. "I'll just be a minute," she said, going out to answer it. "Oh, and help yourselves to a cupcake." She pointed to a dozen golden cupcakes cooling on a rack on the countertop.

Before Mandy had a chance to blink, James was

choosing the biggest one. "I knew this was the perfect job!" he said, grinning.

Carole returned before James could take a bite. "It's for you, Dorothy," she told Gran. "Your husband seems to be having trouble with the instructions you left him for making lunch."

Gran clicked her tongue. "Really! What's so hard about following a recipe for macaroni and cheese?"

While Gran was on the phone, Mandy, James, and Carole started carrying the cakes out to the van. "I bet you'll do well," Mandy said when they were sliding a big box containing an enormous chocolate cake onto one of the racks in the back. "This cake looks incredible. And that cupcake was delicious."

"Thank you," said Carole. "I hope everyone will think so and spread the word."

"I will," said James, who'd just finished a second cupcake. "If I were you, I'd do the first deliveries myself and give everyone I met a cupcake to taste. You'd get hundreds of orders that way."

Carole smiled. "It's a good idea, but I'm too busy right now. You saw how hectic it was in my kitchen. That's why I asked Mandy's grandmother to help me. And, anyway, some of the cakes you're delivering *are* samples."

Mandy and James traded a puzzled look. Carole looked brisk and efficient, but not exactly in the middle of anything. Apart from all the boxes piled up on the table, the kitchen was very tidy. No dirty dishes were lying around and there weren't even any cakes waiting to go into the oven. Carole didn't look too stressed, either. In fact, considering this was her first delivery, she seemed very relaxed.

Maybe she's tired, Mandy decided. *Baking so many cakes must have taken ages.* Back in the kitchen, she checked the delivery list. First stop was a café in Walton, the nearby town where Mandy and James went to school. The second name practically jumped out at her. "Fitzroy Manor!"

Mandy had never been there, but she knew it was a beautiful, big country house on the far side of Walton. It had been owned for centuries by an aristocratic family, the Fitzroys, who held a banquet to benefit charities every Valentine's Day.

"I can't wait to see it," Mandy said. The house wasn't visible from the road and she had only just glimpsed the tree-lined drive beyond the ornate black-and-gold entrance gates.

"You're in for a real treat," said Carole. "It's a spectacular place with rolling lawns, towering oak trees, a lake with a summerhouse on the shore, and a rowboat to take you to the island in the middle." She picked up a cake box and gazed out of the window as if she was picturing the manor. "The house is amazing," she continued. "The entrance hall is the size of a ballroom and the walls are lined with portraits of lords and ladies. And wait until you see the sculpture of a black stallion halfway up the drive. It'll take your breath away."

"It sounds really fancy," said James, polishing off some cake crumbs left on the counter. "Just the kind of wealthy customers you need."

Carole looked around and smiled; Mandy thought her cheeks had turned a bit pink. Maybe she was excited thinking about all her future customers. And yet she had seemed to know an awful lot about the manor, inside and out.

"Do you know the Fitzroys well?" she asked as they carried more boxes of cakes outside.

"Well . . ." Carole began, definitely blushing now. "I knew Edward Fitzroy when we were teenagers."

"Did you go to the same school?" Mandy asked.

Carole opened the back of the van and leaned in to put the cakes inside. "No, we used to date, actually." She backed out again, dusting off her hands. "But it was a long time ago. I expect he wouldn't even remember me now."

"I bet he would," Mandy said, passing her cake box to

Carole. "Maybe you should do the first delivery so you can see him again. You could catch up on old times."

"Goodness me, no," said Carole. "And please, if you see him, don't say anything about me." She took the cakes from James, too, loaded them into the van, then walked back up the path as if she was in a hurry.

Mandy nudged James. "I think she still likes him," she said under her breath.

James rolled his eyes. "Oh, please!" he whispered back. "Stop with that mushy stuff!"

At the door, Carole suddenly turned around. "The thing is, Edward and I stopped dating when he went away to Cambridge University. I wrote to him a few times but he never replied. He must have found another girlfriend."

How terrible! No wonder she doesn't want to see him again, Mandy thought. She couldn't believe someone could have been so heartless. She knew she wasn't going to like Edward Fitzroy at all.

Two

All the way to Fitzroy Manor, Mandy kept thinking about how badly Edward had treated Carole. She wondered what he looked like. Did he have a cruel glint in his eyes and a haughty expression? By the time Gran drove through the gates, Mandy had thought up an image of someone so unpleasant, she didn't want to meet him, not even for a second.

Around the next bend, all thoughts of Carole and Edward vanished when Mandy saw a magnificent black stallion rearing up at the side of the driveway. For a moment, she thought it was real, but she quickly realized it was a statue, the one Carole had mentioned.

"It's incredible!" Mandy exclaimed as Gran slowed down.

The statue was close enough for her to reach out of her window and feel the coolness of the bronze. The stallion towered above her, the head higher than the roof of the van, the expression proud and regal. "It's so lifelike, I feel like I could ride it the rest of the way to the house," Mandy said as Gran drove on again.

The manor turned out to be as amazing as Carole had promised. It was a sprawling white mansion with tall windows, ivy growing up the walls, and a lofty porch supported by graceful stone columns. Surrounding it was a parklike garden, the frost on the lawn glinting like diamonds in the winter sunshine. At the bottom of the slope was the lake, its crystal waters whipped up by the strong wind. Mandy saw the summerhouse Carole had mentioned, and beyond that, fields stretching to the horizon.

Gran stopped the van at the bottom of the steps leading up to the porch. "I hope it's all right to park here," she said anxiously.

While Gran got a box of cupcakes from the back of the van, Mandy and James gazed around. "It's awesome!" Mandy said. But something very important was missing. "But I don't see any animals. You'd think an estate like this would be full of them."

"If I owned the place, I'd have peacocks roaming the grounds and exotic cattle in the fields," said James. "Siamese cats, too, and dogs with shaggy coats and long legs."

"Like Irish wolfhounds," Mandy said. "And don't forget horses, like that stallion."

"There's *got* to be some here," said James. "Maybe they're in the stables because of the frost."

Gran was beckoning to them from the back of the van. "Are you two coming to the front door with me?" She was holding one of the biggest cake boxes.

"Definitely," Mandy said, eager to see inside.

They went up the stairs to the oak-paneled front door, each carrying a box labeled FITZROY MANOR. Mandy rang the brass bell that was so highly polished she could see her own face in it. Moments later, she heard a key being turned in the lock. Imagining aristocratic dogs and aloof Siamese cats, she was rather surprised when the door opened and two fluffy black kittens tumbled out.

Behind them, a woman blinked at Mandy, James, and Gran. "Oh!" she said, as if she hadn't expected to see people carrying pink boxes on the doorstep. And in the same breath, she shouted, "Oh, come back, Meg and Mog!" when she saw the kittens scampering down the steps.

"Got you!" Mandy said, bending down in time to

scoop the nearest kitten up with her free hand. The kitten stared at her with wide eyes.

Meanwhile, James had put down his box and raced down the stairs to catch the other kitten at the bottom. "No, you don't," he said, holding the cute bundle of fluff close to his chest.

"Excellent timing, you two," said the woman with a smile. "Thanks for grabbing them." She was about the same age as Mandy's mom and wore a black skirt and jacket and white blouse. She held a heavy-looking bunch of keys and a clipboard with what looked like a seating chart on it. "All I need today is for those two to get lost. I'm up to my ears as it is."

"Sorry to trouble you, in that case," said Gran. "But this won't take a minute. We've brought some cupcake samples. They're from a new business. . . ." She pointed to the van. Small and pink and with its red-heart logo, it looked rather out of place in front of the imposing entrance. "If you like them, you might want to order some for your Valentine's Day banquet."

"Yes, well, I'm not sure," said the woman. "I'm only the housekeeper, Zena Redman. But do come inside, uh . . ." She looked down at the van. ". . . Carole. I'll see what Lord Fitzroy thinks."

"Actually, I'm not Carole," said Gran. "My name's Dorothy Hope. I'm helping Carole. And these"— she smiled at Mandy and James —"are *my* helpers, Mandy and James."

"So nice to have helpers," agreed Mrs. Redman. She picked up the cake box that James had left on the porch when he'd run after the kitten. "Let me help you with your box, too, Mandy," she said, taking it from her. "It can't be easy juggling a kitten and a box."

Carrying the wriggling kittens, Mandy and James went inside. As Carole had said, the hall was enormous. It had a gleaming white marble floor and dozens of portraits of serious-faced lords and ladies on the wood-paneled walls. The ornate, solid frames matched the jowly faces in many of the paintings. They also matched a very solid-looking brown Labrador curled up on a spindly-legged antique sofa.

"Off, Hobbit," said Mrs. Redman.

Mandy had to stifle a laugh when the burly dog opened one eye, yawned, then went back to sleep.

"Hobbit!" said Mrs. Redman, more firmly this time. "Off!"

Hobbit's eyes stayed shut.

"You're a mischief-maker, aren't you?" Mandy said, tugging on his collar. In her other hand, the kitten squirmed and meowed.

Hobbit opened his eyes, wagged his tail, and licked Mandy's arm, and then the kitten responded with a lightning-fast strike of its front paw on Hobbit's nose. The dog blinked. Mandy thought he looked offended. "Better do as the kitten ordered and get off," she told him.

The dog heaved himself off the delicate sofa and lay down on the floor.

"Well! Who'd have thought it?" said Mrs. Redman, looking impressed. "A word from you and he obeys at once."

Mandy stroked the kitten. "I did have some help."

Mrs. Redman took them through the archway at the back of the hall into a long gallery that had plush Persian carpets on the wooden floor, thick red velvet curtains at the windows, and more paintings on the walls. Mostly, they were portraits like those in the hall, but some showed red-coated huntsmen surrounded by hounds, while in others fine-boned racehorses galloped along a grassy track.

From the gallery, Mrs. Redman led them into a passage that seemed to go on forever. On both sides, open doors gave Mandy and James glimpses of lavishly furnished rooms where the staff was vacuuming, dusting, and polishing. A pair of double doors opened into a vast banquet hall. It was just as well it was so big; the rectangular table that stretched the length of the room was the longest Mandy had ever seen.

"You must be able to get at least fifty people around there," said James.

"Sixty-six, actually," said Mrs. Redman. "With settings for six courses."

Gran blinked. "Imagine having to cook for so many."

A maid was polishing the tall silver candelabra placed at regular intervals down the center of the table. She glanced up, pushing a strand of hair off her forehead. "Oh, Mrs. Redman, we only have fifty starched napkins in ivory. Should we use some white ones as well?"

Mrs. Redman shook her head. "We can't possibly put ivory with white, Annie," she said, sounding exasperated. "There should be more ivory napkins in the linen cupboard next to the blue bedroom upstairs. Find Hodge and ask him to iron them immediately." She hurried on to the next door, where she paused. "I'm sorry if I seem abrupt," she apologized. "It's just that we're so busy today." She opened the door and showed them into the kitchen. It looked bigger than all of Animal Ark. "If you wouldn't mind waiting here a few minutes," she said, going out again. "I'll just see if I can find Lord Fitzroy."

The kittens were struggling to get down. Mandy glanced around and saw a quilted cat bed on the floor under a window. "They might want a nap after their daring escape." She chuckled, lowering her kitten inside it. James put the other one down, too, and the pair snuggled up at once.

Outside, a man in blue overalls was hosing down the cobblestoned courtyard. Another was trimming potted plants that were shaped like lollipops, while a third was on a ladder cleaning windows upstairs.

"It's so busy here," said James, looking through the window. "Imagine keeping a place this big neat and clean. You'd never do anything else."

A loud commotion made Mandy turn around. A blur of gray and black-and-white was barreling toward her in a swarm of legs, whiplike tails, and short glossy coats. "Great Danes!" she exclaimed in delight and sidestepped the gray one before it could bowl her over.

The black-and-white dog made a beeline for James. It was nearly as tall as him. It skidded to a stop and licked his face, dislodging his glasses. James caught them before they slipped off completely. "OK, that's enough," he said, trying to push the dog's massive head away while he struggled to put his glasses back on.

Gran was about to put the cakes on the table but she changed her mind and put them on a shelf out of the reach of swishing tails and long necks. It was just in time, too! The Great Danes suddenly turned and bounded over to her, leaping over each other in their haste to be noticed first. It was like having two spirited ponies in the kitchen.

"You're both magnificent," Gran said, chuckling and putting her hand on their heads to stop them from jumping up. "Now, if you would just calm down for a minute. . . ."

"That's impossible for Horatio and Gilbert," said a red-haired girl about Mandy's age, coming in at that moment. She laughed as the pair kept nudging closer to Gran. "Luckily, they're very gentle," the girl said, and sneezed.

"Gentle giants," Mandy agreed. "Are they yours?"

"No. They're Lord . . ." The girl sneezed again. ". . . Fitzroy's. But they sneak into our apartment on the top floor all the time. My mom's the housekeeper."

"Mrs. Redman?" asked James.

The girl nodded before sneezing again. She took a Kleenex out of her pocket, saying, "This awful flu's kept me out of school for two days already." She blew her nose. "So you know my mom?"

"We met her earlier," Mandy said.

The girl started to speak but another huge sneeze stopped her.

"Bless you, Isobel," said a voice from the door. Mandy looked across and saw a tall man with light brown hair, a warm smile, and eyes as blue as the summer sky. He reminded her of a famous and very handsome actor she'd recently seen in a movie.

"Thank you, Lord Fitzroy," said Isobel, and Mandy stiffened. So this was the man who'd hurt Carole all those years ago.

The Great Danes whirled around and ran to their owner.

"Hi, guys," said Lord Fitzroy, patting them. "I wondered where you were." They sat in front of him and offered him their paws. He smiled and shook both paws before looking up again. "What am I doing, ignoring our visitors? Please forgive me," he said, and came across the kitchen.

Horatio and Gilbert followed him. They clearly adored him. So, too, did Meg and Mog. They'd clambered out of their igloo and were tumbling around Lord Fitzroy's feet.

"I'm Edward Fitzroy," he introduced himself to Mandy, James, and Gran.

Mandy was finding it hard to remember that she had made up her mind not to like him. Her imaginings hadn't prepared her for someone who was handsome, well-mannered, and, most important of all, a big hit with the animals.

Gran had taken the cakes off the shelf. "Thank you for taking the time to see us, Lord Fitzroy," she said.

He smiled at her. "Please call me Edward."

"All right then, Edward," said Gran, who didn't seem surprised that he was so charming. "We've brought some cupcakes for you to sample." She took the lid off the box. The heart-shaped cupcakes inside were small and dainty, topped with the lightest pink icing and with a tiny red cherry in the center. Mandy thought they were exquisite. James looked at them and licked his lips.

"They're a gift from a new business. Home-baked, melt-in-your-mouth, made to order, the best money can buy," Gran reeled off as if she'd been rehearsing the words.

Edward chose one and tasted it. "Mmm, scrumptious. You're right, they're exceptional. I'll buy the whole box."

"No, no," said Gran. "These are a gift. But if you'd like to order more, perhaps for your banquet later this week, do give us a call."

"I'll do that. I'll chat with Mrs. Redman to see how many we need. I hope it's all right to give you short notice," said Edward.

"It'll be fine," said Gran. "I'll warn Carole so that she knows to expect a large order."

"So you're not the owner of the business?" asked Edward.

Gran shook her head. "No. It's Carole . . ." she began, and Mandy mouthed *no* to her in a desperate attempt to

stop Gran giving away Carole's identity. On the way
to the manor, she had filled Gran in about Edward and
Carole.

Luckily, Mrs. Redman came in before Gran could say
anything else. "There you are, Lord Fitzroy," she said.
Hobbit trailed behind her, his nails clicking on the tiled
floor. "So you know about the cupcakes?"

Edward winked at Mandy. "Some people insist on
being formal," he said, and turning to the housekeeper
said, "Yes, my dear Mrs. Redman, I know all about the
cupcakes. All we have to do now is discuss how many
to order."

"All right, but in the meantime, our guest of hon-
or's secretary would like to see you about this
week's arrangements," said Mrs. Redman. "He's in the
library."

"Oh, indeed, the arrangements," said Edward. "We
must figure those out." And bowing slightly to Mandy
and the others, he went out, three dogs and two kittens
following him like a royal entourage.

On the way out the back door, Mandy asked Isobel
about the special guest. Anyone who had a personal
secretary must be very important.

"It's someone very famous," said Isobel, "but I'm not
allowed to say who."

"I bet it's a movie actor or a pop star," said James.
Isobel shook her head.

"A champion soccer player?" James persisted as they turned the corner of the house.

The bright pink van wasn't the only car parked there now. Behind it was a gleaming black limousine with a chauffeur in a gray uniform at the wheel.

"Forget it!" said James. "It can't be a soccer player. They all have sports cars."

"More like the prime minister," Mandy said.

"And we're blocking him in," said Gran, quickening her pace. She nodded to the chauffeur, apologizing for being in the way. "Quick, hop in, Mandy and James," she said as she shut the back of the van and climbed into the driver's seat. A moment later, they roared away, waving out of the windows to Isobel and her mom.

Glancing back at the house, Mandy thought how excited Carole was going to be to hear she'd be catering for a very important person. It was a good thing Gran didn't get a chance to give away her identity. If Edward knew it was the Carole he used to date, he might have changed his mind about the order.

Suddenly, Mandy realized that Edward was about to find out exactly who Carole was. "He'll see her name and phone number on the box!" she gasped. "And he'll put two and two together. Then he won't order the cupcakes after all."

"Of course he will," said Gran, slowing down to drive around a branch the wind must have just blown down. "Carole and Edward must have gotten over their relationship a long time ago. And Edward's not the kind of person who'd refuse to buy something just because of a teen romance."

"He'd be crazy if he did," said James. "Those cupcakes are way too good!"

"I guess you're right, Gran," Mandy said. Now that she'd met Edward, she couldn't imagine him refusing to do business with someone as nice as Carole. And knowing how polite he was, it was a mystery why he'd ignored her letters all those years ago.

The stallion statue loomed up ahead. Mandy was thinking again how real it looked when something very real flashed across the path, missing the van by inches. She barely had enough time to make out what it was before it dove into a tree behind the statue and vanished.

"Did you see that huge bird?" she exclaimed.

"I saw *something*," said James. "I thought it was another branch falling down."

"It was definitely a bird," Mandy said. "And it looked like it was falling, the way it hurtled into the tree."

"It was probably just a pigeon," said Gran. "They do fly rather recklessly."

Mandy looked back, craning her neck as she tried to glimpse it again. "Maybe," she said uncertainly. "But I thought it looked a lot bigger than a pigeon."

It was lunchtime when they finished the deliveries, so Gran dropped Mandy and James at Animal Ark before going on to Carole's. "Oh, Carole said to let you have one of the boxes of leftover cupcakes," said Gran. "To thank you for your help."

"Awesome!" said James, who dashed around to the back.

He opened the door, and Mandy reached in to get the cupcakes. There were a few boxes at the back, on the bottom rack. On the shelf above them, a plastic water bottle was lying on its side, leaking. She could see a gash in it, where the water dripped out. It plopped onto the cake box below. "Oh, no," Mandy said, hoping the cakes weren't ruined. But as she leaned in and pulled the box toward her, she uncovered something soft, furry, and the color of toffee, lying curled up beneath the rack.

"Hey! There's a dog in here," she said to James. The dog had a squat, rectangular body, with a short dense coat and stocky legs. "It looks like a corgi."

"You're kidding . . ." said James, looking over her shoulder, then: "No, you're not. And it *is* a corgi. Where did he come from?"

Mandy shrugged. "I don't know."

Gran came to see what was going on. "A stowaway! We're going to have to retrace our footsteps to find the owner."

Mandy called to the dog. "Wake up, corgi! It's time to go home."

There was no response.

"He's very still," said James.

The corgi *was* still, abnormally still. Dogs didn't usually sleep that soundly, especially when people were moving around nearby and talking.

Mandy clapped her hands to get the corgi's attention. He didn't move. With a sinking heart, she clambered into the van and picked him up. "Oh, no! He's unconscious!" she gasped.

Three

Cradling the corgi in her arms, Mandy shuffled awkwardly on her knees back out of the van. She tried to convince herself that he was just a little under the weather, that he'd wake up soon and be fine, but she knew she was grasping at straws. The corgi was limp and almost lifeless.

"Is he breathing?" murmured James, sliding his arms under the dog's back to help support him.

"Just," Mandy said, seeing his ribs rise slightly.

They headed across the yard to the clinic. Mandy watched the corgi's face for a flicker of an eyelid or a twitch of his nose. Instead, she noticed pink flecks around his muzzle. "Icing?" she wondered out loud, putting her face close to his. She smelled a distinctive sugary aroma. "He's been eating the cupcakes!" As she said this, she caught a whiff of something else. A sharp chemical smell. *Like nail polish remover.*

Gran had dashed ahead of them. "Emily! Adam! It's an emergency," she called, rushing through the waiting room.

Mandy was only vaguely aware of people, and a dog or two, staring at her and James as they hurried after Gran into Dr. Emily's treatment room.

"What happened?" asked Dr. Emily, looking startled.

"I don't know," Mandy said. "We just found him collapsed in the van."

They lowered the corgi onto the examination table and stood back so that Dr. Emily could examine him. Out of the corner of her eye, Mandy saw Gran slip out, closing the door behind her. But it opened again immediately and Dr. Adam came in. "What's up?" he said. Dr. Emily was already listening to the dog's heart with her stethoscope.

Mandy knew that any information could be helpful. "There's icing on his face so he must have been eating the cupcakes."

"Which means he couldn't have been unconscious all that long," added James.

"There's also an odd smell to him," Mandy continued. "Like nail polish remover."

"Icing? Nail polish remover?" Dr. Adam exchanged a look with Mandy's mom.

"Ketones?" said Dr. Emily. She sniffed and raised her eyebrows. "What do you think, Adam?"

"Definitely ketones," he said.

"What are ketones?" Mandy asked, looking anxiously from her mom to her dad. Instinctively, she put her hand on the dog's head as if to protect him from bad news.

Dr. Adam got a catheter and syringe and a bag of intravenous fluid from a cupboard. "They're chemical compounds that a body produces in the blood and urine when it can't use glucose — that's the sugar we need for energy," he explained. "Putting it another way, if there are ketones, it means an animal or human isn't processing glucose properly."

"And what does *that* mean?" asked James.

"That this dog is diabetic," said Dr. Adam. "And that he can't handle sugar. So gobbling up sugary cupcakes didn't do him any good."

Mandy felt relieved. "At least diabetes can be treated," she told James. "He just needs to be given the right medication." She had met several diabetic dogs and cats who were on treatments that allowed them to live perfectly normal lives. The disease involved the body not making enough insulin, the substance that dealt with glucose in the blood. Regular injections of insulin kept the illness under control and the symptoms at bay.

Dr. Emily was feeling the dog's pulse. She glanced at Mandy. "I'm afraid it's not that simple."

Mandy suddenly felt cold.

"It's not only diabetes we have to worry about," Dr. Emily continued. She took a pinch of the skin at the back of the dog's neck, then let it go. The skin stayed pinched. Dr. Emily smoothed it down again. "Just as I thought," she murmured.

"What?" Mandy whispered, feeling more and more alarmed.

"He's dehydrated," said her mom. "Normally, the skin would fall back into place right away. If it stays pinched, it shows the animal is dehydrated."

Mandy thought of the dripping water bottle in the van and remembered that thirst was also a symptom of diabetes. The corgi, desperately thirsty, must have pulled the bottle over and bitten a hole in it to get to the water. But at least dehydration could be treated, too. That's what the bag of fluids and the drip were for.

Dr. Adam was shaving a patch of fur off the corgi's front leg. "Dehydration, the ketone smell, and the dog being unconscious all point to a life-threatening situation. . . ."

Life-threatening? Mandy hadn't expected this.

"It's called diabetic ketoacidosis," said her dad, "or DKA. It happens when too many ketones are produced. That happens in one of two situations, when either the diabetes isn't being treated or it has developed very suddenly. The really worrisome thing about DKA is that it can severely damage the internal organs." He disposed of the razor and wiped the corgi's leg with antiseptic. "If we're going to save this dog, we have to act fast."

"What can I do?" Mandy asked, desperate to help.

"And me?" said James.

"Bring that drip stand over here, James," said Dr. Adam, nodding toward it in a corner. "And Mandy, get me a stick test, please, to check for ketones. You'll find one in the cupboard next to the sink."

Having seen her parents do stick tests for various other conditions, Mandy knew exactly what she was looking for. It was a stick with some colored blobs on it, and a jar with instructions on the side. She found one and took it back to her dad. Dr. Adam had already inserted the catheter into the dog's leg and was drawing blood through it with the syringe.

"Right, let's have a look at this," he said, dipping the stick into the blood. He nodded when he took it out again. "Ketones, as we suspected. My guess is that the diabetes came on very suddenly, especially if it's Type One diabetes."

"Type One?" Mandy echoed. "Are there others?"

"Yep. Type Two develops over time and is seen more often in older dogs, or it's caused by viruses, or a disease called Cushing's disease," said Dr. Emily, going to the drug fridge in the corner. "But Type One is genetic. It's when the pancreas, which produces insulin, doesn't work properly anymore. We usually see it in younger animals, like this little fellow." She took a vial marked INSULIN out of the fridge. "I'd guess he's around eighteen months old."

James had pushed the drip stand to the table. He stood next to Mandy and they watched in silence as Dr. Emily drew some of the insulin into a syringe and injected it into the corgi's shoulder muscle. At the same time, Mandy's dad was attaching the drip to the catheter. "We'll stabilize him first, then start the real treatment as soon as we've got the results of a full blood test," he said. "The insulin will start working right away to lower the levels of glucose in his blood, but we're going to have to monitor those levels to make sure they don't go too low."

"He'll need intensive care," Dr. Emily warned, putting the insulin vial back in the fridge. "I just hope we've caught it in time to prevent his kidneys and liver and other organs being permanently damaged."

Intensive care. Permanently damaged. Mandy stared in dismay at the little body on the table. Lying very still and attached to the drip, the corgi looked so frail. But he was in the best place. Mandy knew her mom and dad were incredible vets; if anyone could help the corgi pull through, they could.

Dr. Adam checked the drip to make sure it was working correctly. "No problems here," he said, and turning to Mandy and James, he added, "there's not a lot more you two can do for the corgi now, so why don't you see how Gran is? She seemed upset when she went out."

Mandy stroked the dog's head one last time. "Poor little boy," she said. "You don't know what's hit you."

"One minute he was enjoying a cupcake, and the next he was out for the count," said James, stroking the corgi's shoulder. "I wish we'd seen him before he got into the cupcakes. Then this wouldn't have happened."

"Not necessarily," said Dr. Emily. "If it is Type One diabetes, it could have come on suddenly at any time. Unless, of course, he's already been diagnosed. So we really need to find out where he comes from."

"Even if his owners don't know about the diabetes, they must be really worried that he's missing," Mandy said. "We'll have to start searching for them right away."

James took out his cell phone. "I'll take a picture of him. Just in case we need to make posters," he said, and took a snap of the unconscious corgi before he and Mandy went out to look for Gran.

They found her in the kitchen, staring at the floor. She seemed as miserable as if the corgi was her own pet. She looked up when Mandy and James came in. "How is the poor little thing?"

Mandy told her all the details.

Gran sighed. "It's all my fault. I shouldn't have left the door open every time we stopped to make a delivery."

"It's not your fault at all," James reassured her. "Dr. Emily and Dr. Adam said he could have gone into a coma at any time."

"We've got to track down his owners," Mandy said. "If you give me the delivery note, Gran, I'll call all the places we went to. He must have come from one of them."

"It's in the van," said Gran. "I'll get it for you, then I'd better head back to Carole. She'll be wondering where I am." She stood up and took the keys out of her coat pocket. "Oh, and by the way, James, while you were with the corgi your mom called to find out where you are."

"Oh, gosh!" said James and looked at his watch. "I'm supposed to be home by now. I promised to take Blackie out while Mom's book club friends are there." Blackie was James's Labrador. He was a large, exuberant dog and not very obedient. "Some of the ladies don't like it when he jumps up on them."

After James and Gran had left, Mandy began her search for the corgi's owners. She was about to dial the first number on the list when her mom came in. "There you are. You can come and see the corgi again. We've stabilized his condition, and Simon's keeping an eye on him."

Mandy put the phone down and went straight to the intensive care room next to the residential unit. The corgi was lying on a soft bed in a roomy enclosure. He was still attached to the drip, and, to Mandy's disappointment, he looked deeply asleep. Simon, Animal Ark's nurse, was sitting in an armchair next to him.

"Any sign of him waking up yet?" Mandy asked.

"Nope," said Simon.

Mandy reached through the wire for the corgi's paw. It was soft and fluffy, oval in shape, with arched toes. It was the foot of a very agile dog. But the dog lying in front of her looked light-years away from ever being fit and agile again, and from ever being able to do what corgis were originally bred to do — herd sheep and cattle. Mandy couldn't bear to think that way. "You *will* get better," she vowed, and squeezed the paw gently in her hand.

Simon stood up to change the drip bag. "I hope you're right, Mandy," he said, unhooking the empty one. "If he makes it, he'll have to be on a strict diet and his owners will need to be very careful about his medication for the rest of his life." He attached the new bag and made sure the fluid was dripping into the catheter before he sat down again.

"I was just going to call around to try and find them," Mandy said.

"Didn't he have a collar and tag?" asked Simon.

"No," Mandy said, but felt around his neck just in case there was a thin one hidden beneath the thick fur. It was the first time she'd really looked at him; until now, the crisis had taken most of her attention. She hadn't noticed that the top of his head was wide and flat between his pricked ears, or that his muzzle was short, and that there was a thin white stripe running down from his forehead to the tip of his black nose. His chest and the ruff under his chin were snow-white, too, so that he looked as if he wore a white shirt beneath a caramel suit. She stroked his head and ran her hand down the back of his neck, noticing there was a white patch there, too. "Look, it's shaped just like a crown," she pointed out to Simon. "So I think I'll call him Little Prince. Just until we know who he really is."

Four

With just eight numbers to call, Mandy was positive that Little Prince's owners would be at his side in no time at all. She started with the last place on the delivery list, certain he must have climbed in there since Gran hadn't noticed him while she was unloading any of the previous boxes. But the people there didn't even own a dog, let alone a corgi. The next place had only a Persian cat, and there were dogs but no corgis at the next four houses. That left only Fitzroy Manor and Sprigs, the café in Walton.

Mandy didn't think Little Prince would have come from Sprigs because it was on busy Main Street, but she dialed the number just to make sure. It turned out that the only pet at Sprigs was a blue parakeet.

"Would you mind putting a sign up in your window?" Mandy said to Astrid who ran the café. "With Animal Ark's number on it, in case the owner sees it?"

"Sure," said Astrid. "I'll make one right away. Oh, and while you're on the phone, we're sold out of cupcakes already. Would you tell Carole we need more? About four dozen this time."

"I'll tell her," Mandy said, making a note on the delivery list. She hung up and dialed the number for Fitzroy Manor. While she waited for someone to answer, she told herself that the stately home was just perfect for a regal corgi nicknamed Little Prince!

"Fitzroy Manor," answered a woman in a voice that made Mandy think of something snapping shut.

"Mrs. Redman?"

"No. Penelope Briggs, Lord Fitzroy's personal assistant. May I help you?" She sounded impatient, like she'd been interrupted in the middle of something important.

"I'm sorry to trouble you," Mandy said, "but we have a very sick corgi at Animal Ark. I think he might belong to Lord Fitzroy."

"No, we don't have a corgi," said Mrs. Briggs.

"Oh, but he . . ." Mandy began.

"I'm afraid I have to go," said Mrs. Briggs. "I just got in from London and I'm very busy." She hung up, leaving Mandy staring into the receiver.

She had called every number, but she hadn't found Little Prince's owners. Yet they had to live *somewhere* near the places she had just called. "We're going to have to retrace our footsteps like Gran said and see if Little Prince belongs to any of the neighbors," she decided out loud.

She called Gran but it was her grandfather who answered. "Sorry, dear, Gran's gone to the Annual General Meeting of the Women's Club. She'll be there for hours. You know how they like to have tea and eat cake after their meetings."

"OK, I'll call her later," Mandy said. Her next call was to Carole to tell her about the Sprigs' order. Carole was out, too, so Mandy left a message on the answering machine.

There was nothing else she could do for the time being so she went to see Little Prince again. There was no change in his condition, and Simon suggested she get some rest while she could. "You might have to do the night shift."

"That's fine," Mandy said, prepared to stay awake all night if it would help. But with the critically ill corgi weighing on her mind, she found it impossible to rest.

She tried to study for her physics test again, but that was just as difficult. In the end, she took supper to the fox in the wildlife enclosure. He'd been found a few days earlier, lying in a ditch with his paw cut. No one could say how it had happened, but Mandy's parents suspected he'd been caught in a snare. There were still cruel people who set traps, even though it was illegal.

When he saw Mandy, the fox darted inside the wooden shelter at the back of his enclosure. Mandy knew not to allow him to get used to her — for their own good, wild animals had to keep their fear of humans — so she put down the bowl of chicken chunks just inside the gate and went away. When she glanced back over her shoulder, she saw him padding silently toward the food. He was still limping, but not nearly as badly as before. *He'll probably be going home tomorrow*, she thought, feeling sorry for the corgi lying indoors. She wished she could be sure he would be going home soon, too.

"He *will* get better!" she said. "And I *will* find his owners."

After dinner that evening, Mandy phoned Gran again. This time she was home, and she said she'd willingly go for a drive the next afternoon to look for the corgi's owners.

Next, Mandy phoned James to update him on Little Prince's condition. "No change," she told him. "Mom and Dad have the results of his blood tests, though."

"So soon?" said James.

"Yes. Luckily they bought a new testing machine last month," Mandy said. "Otherwise we'd have had to send the blood to the laboratory in York and wait a few days to hear the results."

"So what do they show?" asked James.

"They know that it's Type One diabetes, and they know how much glucose is in Little Prince's blood. So now Mom and Dad can give him a treatment plan," Mandy said. "His owners will have to learn everything about controlling his diabetes. Mom says it's different in every patient. Some need injections just once a day, and others need two injections. There are even different types of insulin."

James whistled. "It sounds complicated."

"It's very scientific," Mandy agreed. "So I was thinking it might help if we found out the latest on diabetes and put it all together in a file for Little Prince's owners when we find them."

"Good idea!" said James. "There must be hundreds of sites on the Internet. I'll start searching and print out the best pages and bring them over in the morning."

After hanging up, Mandy went to see Little Prince again. Simon had gone home and Dr. Emily had taken over for him. She was sitting in the armchair doing a crossword puzzle. Little Prince was still asleep.

"Is he any better?" Mandy asked.

Dr. Emily finished filling in a word and said, "It's too early to tell. Now that we've seen what's going on in his blood, we've adjusted his fluids. He's getting potassium, dextrose, phosphate, and bicarbonate. They'll help him, but even if he wakes up soon, he could still have an uphill battle." She yawned and rubbed her eyes. "It's a problem for us not knowing if his diabetes has been diagnosed before and if he's been given treatments for it. If this is the first crisis, then it's unlikely he'll suffer organ damage. But if it's happened before . . ." she said, sighing, ". . . then we could be looking at severe complications. So really, it's a question now of waiting and hoping for the best." She yawned again and pushed her red hair off her face.

Mandy offered to take over. "I'm not very sleepy. And it doesn't matter if I stay awake all night. There's no school tomorrow, remember? I only have to be awake for as long as it takes me and Gran to see if we can find Little Prince's owners."

"I know you'd watch him like a hawk," said Dr. Emily. "But Dad or I should in case his glucose levels drop."

"Can't I monitor that?" Mandy asked.

Mandy's mom shook her head. "It means taking blood every hour."

"That's OK," Mandy said. "I could call you or Dad every hour. You could take it in shifts so that you get two hours' sleep at a time. You can't be awake all night when you have to treat animals the next day."

Dr. Emily paused for a moment and thought, then stood up and stretched. "Are you sure, honey? It'll mean a very long night."

"Even if I went to bed, I'd lie awake all night worrying about him. I might as well stay here next to him," Mandy said.

Her mom hugged her. "Is there anything you won't do to help an animal?"

Mandy smiled. "Probably not."

Armed with an alarm clock set to go off in an hour, and a comforter and pillow that her mom brought her, Mandy curled up in the armchair. She reached out and held Little Prince's paw again. In her other hand, she held her science textbook. If she was going to be awake all night, she might as well use the time to study.

It seemed only moments later that the alarm went off. Mandy's eyes flew open. She'd fallen asleep! She was angry with herself. She looked at Little Prince and breathed a sigh of relief. The regular rise and fall of his

ribs showed he was sleeping peacefully. *What if he'd gone into another crisis*, she wondered, *and I'd slept through it?*

She went upstairs to wake her dad. "Time for the next blood test," she said, shaking his shoulder.

"Oh, right," mumbled Dr. Adam and climbed out of bed.

Back in the intensive care unit, Dr. Adam lifted the fur just above the corgi's tail to reveal a bald patch where his wife had shaved off the hair earlier. She'd done it so that the top coat covered the bare patch.

"Hold the fur back for me please, sweetie," said Dr. Adam.

While Mandy kept the hair back, her dad pushed a slender lancet into the flesh in two places about a half inch apart. Two pinpricks of blood appeared, and he gently squeezed the skin until the drops merged into one. Little Prince didn't even flinch. He must have been deeply unconscious.

Dr. Adam nodded to a strip on the table that looked like the one he'd used earlier in the day to make the diagnosis. "Pass me that please, Mandy."

She gave it to him and he held it under the drop of blood, letting it soak onto the strip. "Now we put this into the glucose monitor," he said, reaching for a gadget that looked a little like a cell phone without a keypad.

He pushed the strip into a slot at the bottom of the monitor. A moment later, a digit appeared on the screen. "So far, so good," he said, and Mandy sighed with relief.

Next, her dad rubbed an herbal ointment into the shaved area. "That's to stop any irritation," he said.

"Is that it?" Mandy said. It seemed an easy enough procedure.

Dr. Adam nodded while he made a note of the reading on Little Prince's chart.

"I could do that," Mandy said.

"You probably could," said her dad. "Lots of young people with diabetes learn to monitor their sugar themselves. They also inject themselves with insulin." He smiled at Mandy. "I know what you're thinking. That you could do the tests and Mom and I can sleep for the rest of the night."

"I wouldn't mind," Mandy said. "But I'd need to practice a few times first."

Her dad gave her a hug. "When this is all over and Little Prince is back home, we'll practice on a toy dog. In the meantime, you're doing a great job as Little Prince's watchdog." He went to the door and glanced back at her. "See you in two hours, Dr. Mandy."

After he'd gone, Mandy switched off the main light, leaving on only a lamp that would allow her to read.

She set the buzzer, then opened her book. "I can't fall asleep this time," she said and looked at Little Prince.

He was looking straight back at her.

"You're awake!" she said, her heart soaring.

The corgi blinked, closed his eyes, opened them, and blinked again. He looked groggy and confused. But he was awake!

"You're wondering where you are, aren't you?" Mandy whispered, stretching across and stroking the side of his face. "Don't worry, you're safe and we're going to make sure you get better."

Little Prince tried to lift his head, but it must have been too much effort because he gave up and put his chin back on his paws.

"It's too soon," Mandy told him. "You're a very sick little dog. Just rest."

As if he understood her, Little Prince breathed out slowly, like he was sighing, and closed his eyes again.

"That's good," Mandy said, smoothing him. "Rest, Little Prince, and get your strength back." And although he didn't respond again, she wasn't disappointed. He'd come out of the coma. He was only sleeping now. *We're over the first hurdle*, she thought.

Five

A ringing noise woke Mandy with a start. She remembered that she was in her own room, and not in the chair next to Little Prince. She'd gone to bed just before dawn, after her mom had insisted she get some sleep.

The noise sounded again. It was the front doorbell. She looked at her watch as she slid out of bed. It was nearly eleven o'clock!

"Half the day's gone," she muttered, annoyed with herself for wasting it sleeping. She went to the window and looked down to see the pink van parked in the driveway.

Grabbing her robe, Mandy ran downstairs and opened the door to find Carole standing on the porch.

"Sorry, Mandy," said Carole, looking surprised to see her still in pajamas. "I didn't know you weren't well."

"I'm fine." Mandy explained why she'd only just gotten up.

"You sat up all night!" Carole said. "That's real dedication."

"It's the least I could do for a special little corgi," Mandy said.

"You must be exhausted," said Carole, following her inside.

"I'm not. And anyway, being a little tired isn't nearly as bad as Little Prince having a crisis again."

Carole looked impressed. "Have you ever thought of becoming a vet?"

Mandy smiled. "Yes. Every day of my life!" Just then, she remembered Astrid's order. "By the way, did you get the message about Sprigs needing more cupcakes?"

"Yes, thank you," said Carole. "It's exactly the kind of repeat order I'd hoped for." She looked as pleased as Mandy had expected her to be. "I've come to ask you another favor, though. Mrs. Redman called half an hour ago. She asked me to stop over at Fitzroy Manor. The Fitzroys want to order a lot of cupcakes for their Valentine's Day banquet."

"That's fantastic!" Mandy said, and wondered why Carole suddenly looked flustered. The Sprigs order hadn't daunted her, so why should this one?

"It *is* a fabulous opportunity," Carole agreed slowly. "And they'll have to be extra-special cupcakes because the guest of honor is a VIP."

Mandy remembered Isobel telling them about the important visitor. "James thinks it might be the prime minister."

"Surely not," said Carole. Although she smiled, she still looked anxious. "I'm on my way to the house now. I was hoping you'd come with me for moral support. It's a bit nerve-racking to have to go there alone."

"Of course I will," Mandy said. Forgetting for a moment that Carole had once known the Fitzroys, she added, "But it's not very formal there. Most of the people are really nice. The animals, too. They've got these really great, uh, Great Danes. We even met Lord Fitzroy!"

The moment Mandy said his name, Carole turned bright red. "Yes, I . . . um . . . well . . ." she stammered. She looked away, folded her arms, dropped them again at her sides, and muttered, "Oh, boy . . ." she turned to Mandy again. "The thing is, I don't want to bump into Lord Fitzroy. Not after all this time. It would be . . . well . . . awkward. I wouldn't know what to say to him."

"*Hello* would be a start, I suppose," Mandy said before racing upstairs to change. Returning a few minutes later, she grabbed a banana for breakfast. "Do you mind if I check on Little Prince before we go?" she asked.

"Of course not," said Carole. "I'd love to see him, too."

In the intensive care unit, Carole bent over the sleeping dog. "What a cutie," she said. "I feel awful about it being my cakes that made him so sick."

"Actually, the cupcakes weren't completely to blame," Mandy reassured her. "Mom and Dad said. The diabetes could have come on suddenly at any time. Even his owners wouldn't have known he was sick until he went into a coma."

"They must be so worried," said Carole. "I know I would be."

Mandy nodded. "Gran and I are going out this afternoon to look for them."

Leaving the corgi sleeping peacefully, they drove away in the pink cupcake van. At Fitzroy Manor, Carole turned off the main driveway just past the stallion statue and followed a narrow road around to the back of the house.

"So there *is* a service entrance," Mandy said as they drew up in the back courtyard. "We parked in the portico yesterday, in front of the main door. When we came out, there was a limousine parked behind us."

"Oh?" was all Carole said. She was looking at her face in the rearview mirror. "I look like a mess!" she said, loosening her hair.

"No, you don't," Mandy said.

"I do," said Carole. She started rummaging in her handbag. "There's got to be some lipstick and mascara in here," she said, giving up when she found only the lid from a lipstick tube. "And look at my jeans. There's a butter stain on them!" She slumped back in her seat and raised her hands in despair. "I should have dressed better. Edward . . . I mean Lord Fitzroy . . . will think I'm just a local girl who never got anywhere. That I missed out on all the chances I had to make something of my life."

Mandy saw the kitchen door open and Mrs. Redman come out. "But you look just fine. And you have gotten somewhere," Mandy said as she and Carole climbed out of the van. "You have a lot to be proud of." She pointed to the heart-shaped logo on the side. She glanced at Carole and thought again how pretty she was with her hair falling in soft waves around her shoulders and her lovely blue eyes that were a few shades darker than her blue sweater. "If anyone's missed out," Mandy ventured, "it's Lord Fitzroy."

"Never," said Carole. "He must have everything he ever wanted. Mrs. Redman?" she called, abruptly changing the subject and heading toward the back door. "I'm Carole."

In the kitchen, Mrs. Redman sat down at the table with Carole to discuss the cupcake order. Mandy looked around for the dogs and Meg and Mog, but was disappointed when she saw they weren't there.

"We'll need at least five dozen," Mrs. Redman was saying to Carole. "We're hoping you can come up with something sophisticated but with a romantic theme, and that fits in with the family crest."

"I've been thinking about that," said Carole, "and last night, I worked on a few ideas." She turned to the back of her order book and showed Mrs. Redman some sketches. "What about a tiny red rosebud on each cupcake?"

"How lovely," said Mrs. Redman. "And it's a lot like the rose in the family crest. Look there." She pointed to a framed tapestry that Mandy hadn't noticed the other day. It was in the shape of a shield with an old-fashioned knight's helmet on top and a scroll with FITZROY in red capital letters on the bottom. Curling red-and-white fronds that reminded Mandy of ostrich feathers framed the shield. In the center was a wide red band in an upside-down V. Below that was a black stallion exactly like the one next to the driveway. There was a blue star in the top left corner and a white swan in the top right corner and between them, a perfectly formed red rosebud.

"It's quite a coincidence you came up with a rose identical to the one in the family crest," said Mrs. Redman. "One would think you'd seen it before."

"Well . . ." Carole began, but stopped when the door burst open and the Great Danes galloped in.

"Horatio and Gilbert!" Mandy laughed as they ran to her, wide doggy grins on their faces.

"What gorgeous dogs," said Carole.

Hobbit plodded in behind them, his tail wagging slowly from side to side and his head drooping as if he were too lazy to hold it up.

"Hi, Hobbit," Mandy said. "You look like you just woke up. But your brothers look like they're ready to rock and roll!"

"It sounds like you've known them for years," came a familiar voice from the door. "The rockers and the . . ."

Edward Fitzroy broke off and stared across the room, at Carole.

Silence engulfed the kitchen. Even the dogs grew quiet. Mandy heard Carole catch her breath, and saw her look down at her order book and pretend to focus on the rosebud sketch. Mrs. Redman frowned at Edward, glanced at Carole bent over her book, and looked back at Edward, her eyebrows raised in a silent question.

Mandy waited for someone to speak, to break the icy atmosphere. Edward seemed frozen, and Carole too nervous to look him in the eye. Or was she angry? Edward was probably mad, too, at finding her in his house. Carole said he'd never answered her letters. There may have been a lot more to it, though. They might have argued all those years ago and parted on angry terms.

Mandy wished she could go outside. Someone was bound to speak soon and that could lead to a new argument. Mandy hated listening to adults fighting.

Near the back door, Horatio and Gilbert started to butt each other playfully. Any moment and they'd be charging around like football players. Mandy saw her chance; she'd offer to take the dogs out to stretch their legs. She opened her mouth to speak but it was Edward's voice that suddenly broke the silence.

"Carole?" he said. "I can't believe it." He didn't sound angry at all.

Carole looked up at him. "Hello, Edward . . . I mean, Lord Fitzroy," she said, her cheeks burning.

"I, uh . . ." Edward faltered. "It's been a long time."

"A very long time," agreed Carole, covering her cheeks with her hands as if she was trying to cool them.

"Do you know each other?" asked Mrs. Redman, sounding puzzled.

No one answered her. Carole and Edward kept staring at each other. More than ever, Mandy wasn't sure what to do or where to look. It was a good thing that James wasn't there. He'd be squirming like a snake by now.

"It's been what . . . ten years?" said Edward, ignoring Hobbit who was pawing at his leg to get his attention.

Carole shook her head. "Thirteen."

Edward frowned. "Never!"

"It has," said Carole, and looked away.

Edward took a step forward, stopped, looked down, and then at Carole. "Thirteen years." He shrugged. "And in all that time I . . ." He broke off and took a deep breath.

Mandy wanted to fade into the wallpaper. This was getting really embarrassing.

"Look, I should go," Edward said abruptly. "Excuse me." He dashed out in a hurry.

"What was that all about?" demanded Mrs. Redman.

"It's nothing," said Carole, still blushing. Picking up her pen, she made a note in her order book. "You said five dozen cupcakes, on cake stands, and decorated with red rosebuds, didn't you?"

Carole was silent for most of the journey home. She gripped the steering wheel and concentrated on the road ahead. Mandy tried to break the silence by offering to help her with the two big orders. "I'm sure James will help, too," she said. "We'll come over tomorrow morning if you want."

"That's very kind of you," said Carole and fell silent once more. It was only when she pulled up in the driveway at Animal Ark that she spoke again. "So much for that, then."

"You mean your meeting with Lord Fitzroy?" Mandy asked.

"It couldn't have been more disastrous," Carole sighed.

"Why do you say that?"

Carole stared at the garage door. "You saw what happened. He was horrified when he saw me. The way he rushed out of that kitchen, it was obvious he couldn't wait to get away from me. Just like when he went to Cambridge."

"Really?" Mandy had a different picture altogether. Carole and Edward *had* been surprised to see each other again. But they'd stammered and blushed and, as far as Mandy was concerned, generally carried on like . . . well, just like ten-year-old Rachel Farmer when she'd had a huge crush on James.

After Carole had driven away, Mandy went to see Little Prince. She bumped into James and Gran coming out of the intensive care unit.

"Poor little fellow," said Gran, "hooked up to a drip like that." She took her car keys out of her pocket. "I hope we find his owners quickly. Are you two ready to leave?"

Mandy hadn't expected Gran until the afternoon. Then she realized it *was* the afternoon. Waking up at eleven had really messed up her day.

"I'll be ready as soon as I've been in to see him," Mandy said.

James couldn't join them on the search, unfortunately. "I've got to help Dad clean out the garden shed."

"Can't you get out of it?" Mandy asked.

"I tried, but he won't let me," said James. "It was Blackie who made the mess."

After checking on the corgi, who was awake but didn't seem to want to move very much, Mandy set off with Gran. They were headed for the second place on the delivery list; a house a couple of miles outside the village on the road to Walton, since Fitzroy Manor didn't have any neighbors where the corgi could have come from. Gazing through the window as they sped along, Mandy felt sad when she saw a man and three lively brown-and-white spaniels walking through a field.

"Little Prince should be out walking with his owner, too," she murmured.

Just then, a dark, arrow-shaped figure swooped past them. "It's that bird again! And it's definitely not a pigeon," she said as it dove across the road, pushed by the strong wind.

It was headed straight into the path of a massive truck!

Six

"It'll be killed!" Mandy screamed.

The truck slammed on its brakes, but it still hit the bird. The truck jerked to a stop and the bird slid limply from the hood and landed on the road.

Gran braked and Mandy flung her door open.

"Watch out for other cars!" she heard Gran yell as she sprinted across the road. Luckily there was only a motorcycle coming over a hill in the distance. It roared past as Mandy reached the other side of the road and crouched next to the bird.

It lay on the ground, a crumpled heap among scattered loose feathers. One wing was stretched out at an awkward angle like it was broken, and the head was twisted back.

The driver came around from the cab. He was young, probably about twenty-five. "It came out of nowhere," he said, pushing his cap back from his forehead. "I didn't see it until it was too late." He kneeled next to Mandy. "It's dead, isn't it?"

Mandy nodded.

"What sort of bird is it?" asked the driver.

"I don't know," Mandy admitted. It was a dark grayish-brown, and large — much bigger than any pigeon — but with a narrow head that *was* a little like a pigeon's. The beak was black and slender and there were dense feathers on the face.

"It didn't stand a chance." Mandy sighed as she gazed down at the fragile, broken, but still very beautiful body. The legs and feet were yellow, and there were two broad dark bars at the base of its long tail and another at the tip. Flecks of brown made the white underparts look as if they had been stroked with a paintbrush. As Mandy admired the subtle markings, she suddenly thought she saw the bird's chest rise and fall. She held her breath and waited, hoping she wasn't just imagining things.

There it was again, the slightest movement of the ribcage. "It's not dead!" Mandy whispered as her grandmother came over. "It's just stunned."

Gran bent down between Mandy and the driver. "I think I can see it breathing."

Mandy didn't allow herself to get her hopes too high. "It looks like its wing's broken, though."

The driver rocked back onto his heels. "We've got to get it to a vet fast. Is there one near here?"

Mandy and Gran exchanged a glance. "Yes. Animal Ark," Mandy said. "My mom and dad are the vets there." The mission to find Little Prince's owners would have to be put on hold. Another creature was in critical condition. But getting the bird to Animal Ark wasn't going to be easy. "It might start struggling when we pick it up. It could hurt itself even more," Mandy said.

"We could wrap it in something," said the driver. "I've got a first-aid kit in the truck. Let's see what's in there."

The kit contained a roll of wide gauze bandage. "We could strap the wing close to the body with this," Mandy suggested. As carefully as she could, she folded the wing back against the bird's side. "So far, so good," she murmured and eased her hands beneath the bird to lift it so that Gran could wind the bandage around it.

To Mandy's relief, the bird didn't even try to resist. She was surprised at how little it weighed considering it was such a big bird. *Less than two pounds*, she thought. *Probably only seventeen or eighteen ounces.* While Mandy cradled it in her arms, watching for a flicker of its eyes that would hint that it was waking up, Gran wound a length of the gauze around its middle, strapping the injured wing against its side but leaving the other one free. "There," she said, tucking in the end. "That should do until we get it to the clinic."

"But in case it does start struggling, you could put this around it," said the driver, and he pulled off his sweater. "Wrap it up snugly," he said, giving it to Mandy. "It's angora, so it'll keep it warm."

"Angora, huh?" murmured Gran, feeling the sweater and raising her eyebrows. She looked at the driver in his sleeveless T-shirt. "We'll give it back to you as soon as we reach Animal Ark."

He waved his hand. "Don't worry, I'll pick it up in a few days. Where is Animal Ark?"

While Mandy wrapped the bird safely in the sweater, Gran gave the driver directions to the clinic.

"I'll see you in a day or two," he said, crossing the road with them. He held Mandy's door open while she climbed in with her fragile bundle, and helped her fasten her seat belt.

Driving as fast as she dared, Gran covered the few miles back to Animal Ark in minutes. There, Mandy charged through reception, carrying the swaddled bird in her arms. Behind her, Gran called out, "Come quickly. It's another emergency!" and Dr. Adam appeared on the threshold of his treatment room, asking what had happened.

It was almost an exact rerun of the day before.

Only this time, it's a different creature altogether, Mandy thought, going into her dad's room.

"It flew into a truck," she said as she laid the bundled-up bird on the table.

Her dad raised his eyebrows. "And it's still alive?"

"Barely. I think its wing's broken," Mandy said. With that, the bird suddenly opened its eyes, and Mandy saw that its irises were an unusual orange color. It blinked a few times and looked around, but stayed very still on the table.

Dr. Adam unwrapped the sweater as if he was folding back the petals of a delicate flower. Mandy saw a slight ruffling of the feathers on the bird's back and neck when it was freed from its angora cocoon.

Dr. Adam whistled in surprise. "It's a raptor," he said, just as Dr. Emily came in.

"What species is it?" she asked. "It's nothing like the birds of prey we get in Yorkshire."

"It's a honey buzzard. A male. You can tell by the orange irises," said Dr. Adam, who was an avid bird-watcher. "And you're right, Emily. These birds aren't normally found here." He examined the buzzard, checking it for injuries. "This wing's in good shape at least," he said, extending the unstrapped one.

Mandy was astonished at how big the wingspan was. It must have been more than a yard long!

"Let's look at the other one," said Dr. Adam, carefully unwinding the gauze bandage.

At once the buzzard started to struggle, flapping his massive wing and making it difficult for Mandy's dad to hold him.

"Hold him by the wrist, please, Emily," he said.

Mandy was surprised when her mom held the bony part of the wing where it folded back near the top of the bird's body. "I thought that was the shoulder," she said.

"I suppose when the wing's closed, this part does look like a shoulder," said Dr. Emily. "But stretched out, it's more like where a wrist is, if you compare it with a human arm."

With his wrist restrained, the bird stopped fighting. He looked thoroughly miserable, though, lying on the table with his legs folded beneath him. He must have been terrified, surrounded by people holding him down and prodding him all over. *How different he must be in flight*, Mandy thought, and she imagined him soaring with both wings extending a yard on each side.

Dr. Adam had taken off the bandage. "There's no obvious fracture," he said, examining the wing. "What made you think it was broken, Mandy?"

"It was at an awkward angle."

Gran nodded. "I saw it, too. It was splayed out, and made me think of the time you broke your arm when you were twelve, Adam."

Dr. Adam slowly stretched the wing out. "It might have just been knocked into that odd angle when he fell."

"I hope that's all it was," Mandy said. "A broken wing must mean serious trouble for birds."

"Very serious trouble," agreed her mom, "especially for raptors. If the wing doesn't heal properly, it affects the bird's hunting skills. You've seen birds of prey swooping and diving to catch their food, haven't you, Mandy?"

She nodded.

"A damaged wing would mean the bird couldn't balance itself properly or dive accurately when going after its prey," said Dr. Emily. "Unfortunately, that could mean it would starve to death."

Dr. Adam took over from Mandy's mom and held both of the bird's wrists. "The other thing about a wing fracture," he said, "is that we'd have to give the bird a general anesthetic so that we could set the bone. But anesthetics are very risky for birds and it's not easy to get them to wake up afterward."

"I suppose we could say that this is one lucky bird, to have gotten away with no broken bones," said Dr. Emily.

Mandy felt her spirits lift. "Does that mean we can let him go?"

"Well, not right away," said Dr. Emily, examining the bird's throat and chest. "There are all these other injuries from the accident." She pointed out some cuts and scratches on his chest and several more on his belly. "They'll need time to heal. There's probably also severe internal bruising. We're going to have to keep an eye on him for a while."

"And I'm not sure about releasing him in an area where he shouldn't even be," said Dr. Adam.

"Where *should* he be?" asked Gran.

Before Mandy's dad could answer, Jean Knox opened the door. "We're getting a little crowded out here," she said. "Should I ask people to come back later?"

"No. We'll start seeing them in a few minutes. We're just going to give the bird a shot of antibiotics; then we'll put him in the wildlife unit," said Mandy's mom. She prepared the syringe while Dr. Adam cleaned the buzzard's cuts and scratches with disinfectant.

Mandy went to the storeroom to get a roomy

birdcage that was usually used for exotic birds like parrots. *Who would have thought a wild bird of prey would also need it?* she thought as she carried it back to her dad's treatment room. She put it on the table, lined it with clean newspaper, and filled up the water dispenser.

"In you go, big boy," said Dr. Adam. He put the honey buzzard onto the floor of the cage, and Mandy closed the door.

When they took the bird into the indoor section of the wildlife unit, Mandy's dad turned up the thermostat. "He should be in Africa right now," he said, "so we'd better make it as tropical in here as possible."

"He's from Africa?" Mandy asked, amazed.

"That's where honey buzzards spend the winter," said her dad. "They're migratory birds."

"Then I think we should call him Nomad," Mandy said. "After the tribes of people who move from place to place." She'd have liked to learn more about the beautiful raptor, especially why he was so far from his winter habitat, but there was no time to talk right then. The next patient was already in her dad's treatment room.

There was, however, another pressing puzzle for Mandy to solve. "Should we get back to our search for Little Prince's owners, Gran?" she asked, going into

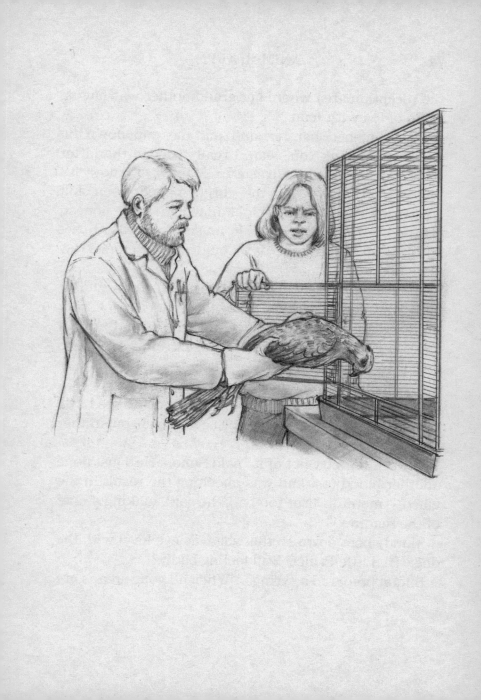

the reception area where her grandmother was having a cup of tea with Jean.

Gran finished her tea and put the cup down on the desk. "Thank you, Jean. I really needed that after all the drama." She turned to Mandy. "I know it's important that we find the corgi's people soon, but it's getting close to five o'clock now and, to be honest, I'm not feeling very well. It must be all the upset with these poor animals. Could we go tomorrow instead?"

Mandy realized her grandmother did look kind of pale. And come to think of it, she suddenly felt very tired herself. "That's all right, Gran," she said. "But we'll have to go after lunch. James and I promised to help Carole in the morning."

"Then I'll pick you up at about two," said Gran.

After Gran had driven away, Mandy went to see Little Prince. He lay on his side, his eyes open but rather glazed.

"He's still pretty out of it," said Simon. He'd just done another blood test and was checking the result in the glucose monitor. "Not too bad," he said, making a note of the reading.

Mandy bent down so that she was eye level with the dog. "Hi, Little Prince. Still feeling badly?"

Simon prepared a syringe. "When all your organs are

as sick as his must be, you wouldn't even want to wake up." He injected the medication into Little Prince's shoulder muscle.

"Insulin?" Mandy asked.

"Uh-huh," said Simon. "Just part of his daily routine now."

"And for the rest of his life," Mandy said. "We have to make sure his owners understand that it's the only way he can stay healthy."

"The honey buzzard looks a little better. He tried to peck my fingers when I changed his water," Mandy told James the next morning.

They were at Carole's house helping her with the orders. Carole had stayed up late the night before, baking batches of cupcakes and making dozens of perfect-looking red-icing rosebuds. The next step was to cover the cakes with white icing and place the dainty roses on top.

Wearing thin plastic gloves, Mandy picked up a rosebud and put it carefully in the center of a cupcake. "That looks stunning," she said, standing back to admire it. "Lord Fitzroy will be very impressed."

Carole stood at the counter, mixing up more white icing. "I hope so. But you never know. People like Edw — Lord Fitzroy are used to having only the best. He'll probably find something wrong with the cupcakes."

"I don't see how he could," said James, taking off his glasses. The lenses were smeared with white icing.

"You're supposed to put the icing on the cupcakes," Mandy teased, "not on your glasses."

James pulled a face. "I'm not used to cooking," he said. He wiped his glasses on a towel and put them back on.

"You're doing very well," said Carole. She went to the fridge and took out the milk. "Time for a break. Who'd like a cup of hot chocolate?"

"I would, please," said James. "A cupcake, too, if there's one to spare!" He looked hungrily at the boxes of completed cupcakes occupying every surface.

"Of course there's one to spare. Two or three if you like." Carole smiled, pouring milk into a saucepan. She stopped and listened. "Who's that?"

Mandy listened, too, and heard a car engine. It was very close, like it was just outside. It spluttered once or twice then cut out. "Someone in a car that's broken down?" she suggested. She heard a door creak open, then slam shut.

"It could be someone coming to place another order," said James.

"I hope not," said Carole, going over to the window. "At least not until I've gotten these two out of the way." She looked outside. "Oh, no!" she gasped and ran out of the kitchen and up the stairs with the milk jug still in her hand.

"What's going on?" said James, dropping a rosebud into the bowl of white icing.

Mandy crossed to the window. An old car was parked in the drive. Once, the paint would have been a sparkling white, but the shine had long gone. Now, the car was dull and almost beige except for one front wing that was a faded red. There were dents in both front doors, and a rusty patch on the hood. *What a wreck.* It looked like it belonged on a scrap heap.

The front doorbell rang. Carole called down from upstairs, "Would one of you get the door, please? And say I won't be long."

Mandy went into the hall. "Coming," she said when the bell rang again. She opened the door.

Edward Fitzroy stood on the doorstep.

Seven

"Oh, um . . . the cupcakes aren't quite ready," Mandy said.

"I didn't come for them," said Edward, looking past her. "I've . . . come to buy a cake. For . . . my mother."

"Oh, I see," Mandy said, but what she really saw was how nice he looked; tall, sophisticated, and trendy — a complete contrast to the funny little car outside. He wore black jeans, ankle-high leather boots, and a snug-fitting, cream V-necked sweater.

"I thought, while I was out, I could, um . . . have a look at the cupcakes, too!" he said, still peering past Mandy.

"I guess that's all right. . . ." Mandy began.

Hearing a slight noise behind her, she turned around. Carole was at the bottom of the stairs. She had changed out of her stained apron, baggy sweatshirt, and jeans into a pale yellow dress with long sleeves and a swirly skirt. Her hair was loose and shining as if it had been brushed a thousand times. In the few minutes she'd been upstairs, she'd even managed to put on some makeup.

"Hi, Carole," said Edward, his voice sounding rather strained. "I hope you don't mind me arriving out of the blue like this."

Mandy glanced at Carole and saw that she was blushing. *She doesn't mind*, Mandy thought; it was obvious that Edward was very impressed with her outfit.

"I see you came in Beulah," said Carole, her voice almost a whisper.

"You remember her?" said Lord Fitzroy, glancing over his shoulder. Mandy guessed that Beulah was the old car.

Carole nodded. "Who could forget?"

There was a pause. It went on so long, Mandy started to feel uncomfortable.

"So, what brings — ?" began Carole, while Edward said, "I was, uh —"

They stopped, each waiting for the other to go on.

"You were saying?" said Carole when Edward didn't continue.

"Yes, I was just passing," said Edward, "on my way to . . . to the gym."

Which gym? Mandy wondered. The nearest one was miles away from Carole's house, in Walton.

"And I'd like to buy a cake," Edward continued, a little too abruptly.

"But we're busy making cakes for your banquet," said Carole, her cheeks still burning.

"Yes, I know. That's why I'm here. To have a look at them."

Mandy tried not to smile.

"You know, to see if they're . . ." Edward stammered.

"Suitable?" said Carole, raising her eyebrows.

"No, I'm sure they're wonderful," said Edward. "But a sneak preview would be nice."

"All right then," said Carole.

In the kitchen, James had fished the rosebud out of the bowl. Globs of white icing had stuck to it, and he was trying to clean them off. Edward gave him a sympathetic look. "Tricky job."

Carole smiled. "Don't worry about it. I've made extras." She took the lid off one of the boxes and revealed the dainty cupcakes decorated with tiny rose-buds nestling on beds of white icing.

Edward whistled. "That's what I call art." He looked directly into Carole's eyes. "Perfectly romantic cakes for a very romantic occasion made by a perfectly clever person."

Mandy sneaked a look at James, who rolled his eyes.

"I've had a lot of help," said Carole. "Mandy and James did all the decorations."

"Keep up the good work, James," said Edward. He turned and bowed to Mandy. "You've done a great job, too, young lady."

Mandy hoped *she* wouldn't start blushing next.

"They're both very talented young people," said Carole hastily. "Mandy's great with animals, too. You should ask her about the honey buzzard she just rescued. And the corgi she and James saved." She put the lid on the box and looked around, muttering, "What did I do with the milk?"

Edward had been gazing at Carole in a fuzzy sort of way, but he turned to Mandy and frowned. "A corgi?"

"He was in a diabetic coma," Mandy said. "So we rushed him to Animal Ark."

James was licking icing off his fingers. "Little Prince

was in Carole's van after we delivered those cakes to your house."

Edward watched Carole go to the fridge and take out another bottle of milk. "Little Prince, eh?" He shook his head. "Then it's definitely not him."

"Definitely not who?" Mandy asked.

"The corgi we're looking for," said Edward. "He disappeared two days ago. We've hunted everywhere for him. In fact, my staff are still searching the fields."

Mandy caught her breath. "What does he look like?"

"Caramel colored, with a white stripe down his nose, a white bib, and a white patch at the back of his neck," said Edward.

"The white patch on his neck — is it shaped like a crown?" Mandy checked.

Edward thought for a moment, then nodded. "I suppose it is, yes."

"Little Prince!" Mandy burst out. The search for his owners was over. "It must be the same one."

Edward shook his head. "I don't think so. His name's Condor."

"But Little Prince is just a nickname I gave him," Mandy said. "We didn't know where he came from."

"And we found him the same day your corgi disappeared," said James. "*After* we'd been to your house."

"Really?" said Edward. He folded his arms and frowned. "I must say, it does kind of add up. We'll have to make sure, of course. . . ."

"That's easy," said James. "I took a picture of him with my cell phone and downloaded it onto my computer. I could e-mail it to you as soon as I get home so you can show your friend."

"Good idea," said Edward. He gave them his e-mail address and then smiled at Mandy and James. "If your Little Prince *is* Condor, Kate's going to be so relieved."

"Kate?" said Carole, putting the bottle down so hard that milk splashed out onto the countertop.

"Kate's a guest," said Edward. "She and Condor have been staying at the manor for a few days."

Mandy saw a look of disappointment on Carole's face; she had a similar sinking feeling inside. *Kate must be Edward's girlfriend.*

Edward got a cloth from the sink and wiped up the spilled milk for Carole. He was rinsing out the cloth again when he said, "But if that corgi is diabetic, he can't be Condor. Kate didn't mention anything about him being sick."

"That's just it," Mandy said. "We don't think his owners know he's got diabetes. He went into a DKA coma very quickly, which means he's probably not on insulin treatment."

Edward looked impressed with how much Mandy knew. But he also seemed alarmed. "Diabetic? If he *is* Condor, his owner is going to be devastated to hear how ill he is."

"It's no good being devastated," said Carole, pouring milk into a saucepan. "This Kate is going to have to learn how to care for her dog correctly. And to keep an eye on him so he doesn't wander off in unfamiliar places." Her sudden brisk tone made Mandy and James exchange another glance.

Edward must have noticed it, too. He raised his eyebrows and looked a bit surprised. "No, you've got it wrong," he said. "Kate's not . . ."

Mandy waited for him to say *"my girlfriend."*

"Condor's owner," Edward continued. "She was just looking after him for . . . someone else. Kate had to go back to London early this morning on urgent business, but she's very worried about Condor." He looked at his watch. "She'll be in her office now. I'd better get home. The sooner I get in touch with her, the better."

"Well, of course," Carole said crisply, switching on the stove.

Mandy found a pen and wrote down Animal Ark's telephone number on a piece of paper. "This is where Condor's owner can contact Mom and Dad."

"His owner and Kate will be at the banquet," said Edward. "So I could bring Kate over that afternoon. We could even pick him up then if he's ready to go home."

"I can't say if he will be," Mandy said. Valentine's Day was just two days away. "His owners will have to speak to Mom and Dad."

"We'll figure it out," said Edward. He went over to Carole, who was watching the saucepan, waiting for the milk to boil. "I'm sorry to rush off." Her back was to him. He lifted his hand and for a moment Mandy thought he was going to touch Carole's shoulder. But he dropped his hand again. "Lovely. The cupcakes, I mean. Thank you for the sneak preview."

Carole nodded but didn't turn around. "That's all right, Lord Fitzroy." She sounded tense and angry, a very different Carole from the friendly person Mandy was getting to know. And very different from the Carole who had dashed upstairs in a panic to change when she'd seen her old boyfriend arriving.

It was the mention of Kate that had changed things.

And yet Edward seemed crazy about Carole. He'd hardly taken his eyes off her the whole time he'd been there. *Grown-ups can be so complicated*, Mandy thought.

A few minutes later, hearing the dented jalopy that was Beulah sputtering off down the road, she realized that Edward had gone away empty-handed. He'd never meant to buy a cake for his mother after all! It *was* just an excuse. *Edward definitely stopped by to see Carole*, she thought. And it was good that he did. It looked like they'd found Little Prince's owner!

Eight

"Good news, Gran," Mandy said, running outside to meet her that afternoon. "Little Prince is actually named Condor and we don't have to go hunting for his owners. We found them! If everything goes well, he'll be back with them by Valentine's Day."

Gran climbed out of her car. "What a splendid Valentine's gift that will be! How did you find his family?"

Mandy told her about Edward's surprise visit to Carole that morning; James had e-mailed a picture of Condor to him since then. "Lord Fitzroy called a little while ago to say it definitely was the same corgi. He didn't actually say who the owners are, though," she finished. "But Kate will tell them everything."

"Let's hope they'll take proper care of Condor from now on," said Gran. "And not let him wander off, especially with him having diabetes."

"Lord Fitzroy says they'll be shocked to hear what's happened to him," Mandy said. "And just in case they don't know about diabetes, James and I are going to put together an information pack for them."

"Good idea," said Gran. "How is Little Prince, anyway?"

"You mean Condor." Mandy smiled. "Mom says he's a little better. I was just going to see him now."

"I'll come, too," said Gran.

Condor was still attached to the drip but he was completely awake at last. To Mandy's delight, he wagged his stubby tail when he saw her.

"That's the first time you've given me a doggy smile," Mandy said, stroking him. He wagged his tail again and licked her hand. "Keep this up, and you'll definitely be home for Valentine's Day," she said.

Gran patted Condor, too. "It's lovely to see you looking better. But remember, little fellow, no more cupcakes."

Condor blinked at her. He looked as innocent as the day he was born, as though it would never enter his head to steal a cupcake.

But there was little to celebrate when they went in to see the honey buzzard. With his head drooping between his shoulders, he looked utterly miserable as he stared out through the bars at the walls of the wildlife unit.

"Poor guy, you must be wondering what happened to the sky," said Gran.

"I'd like to know why he's here in Yorkshire," Mandy said. All she knew so far was what her dad had told her about honey buzzards being migratory. "By the way, Gran, I've named him Nomad."

"Lovely name," said Gran as they went out to the enclosure where the fox had been. He'd been released that morning, and Mandy had promised to clean out the enclosure. "Why did you choose it?"

"Because he really is a nomad. He's a migratory bird," Mandy said. "Or, he's *supposed* to be one." She went inside the enclosure to get the feeding bowls. "We just don't know what he's still doing in England. He should be in Africa by now."

Gran followed and shook out the bedding in the wooden shelter. "I'm sure you'll figure out that mystery soon, just like you've solved the corgi one."

"I don't know," Mandy said. "Nomad probably doesn't have any owners looking for him who can tell us what happened."

They went into the utility room next to the wild-life unit. Gran pushed the bedding into the washing machine, while Mandy scrubbed the dishes in the sink.

"There's something else that needs to be worked out," Mandy said.

Gran switched on the washing machine. "What's that?"

"Carole and Edward's relationship."

The gushing noise from the washing machine as it started drawing in water must have drowned Mandy's voice because Gran looked around, frowning. "What did you say?"

"Carole and Edward," Mandy repeated. "I think they like each other. I mean, *really* like each other."

Gran gave Mandy a warning look. "Mandy Hope, you're not planning what I think you're planning, are you?"

Mandy dried the bowls and put them on a shelf. "I'm not planning anything." In a small voice, she added, "Yet." She hung up the dishcloth. "But someone should do something to get them back together."

"Just as I thought," said Gran, her expression even more stern. "That someone, no doubt, is you."

"Well . . ." Mandy began.

Gran put her hands on her hips. "Don't interfere, Mandy. Grown-ups don't like other people arranging their private lives for them."

"I'm not," Mandy insisted. "I'm just trying to think how to help them . . . you know, realize they still love each other. It's the perfect time."

"No," said Gran. "Valentine's Day is not the time to make serious decisions. People let their emotions run wild. They make silly promises that get broken as quickly as the chocolates are eaten and the flowers have wilted." A tinny, electronic tune broke out, making Gran jump. "Oh, my!" she said and fumbled in her pockets, pulling out a tiny silver cell phone. She stared at it as if it was a loaded weapon, then flipped it open. The tinny tune stopped. "Hello," she said very loudly, holding the phone about six inches from her ear. "Yes, Dorothy here." She was practically shouting. "All right. Will do. Be there in ten minutes. Over and out." She closed the phone. "I'll have to go. Muriel needs a hand with pricing items for the Women's Club Red Heart Valentine Crafts Day."

"Items like chocolates and flowers?" Mandy teased. Gran chuckled.

"When did you get the phone, Gran?"

"This morning. Grandad gave it to me. He said it

would make it easier for me to organize the crafts fair. But I think he's just sick of answering calls from the club ladies," said Gran with a twinkle in her eye. "He never said as much, of course. He told me it was an early . . ."

"Valentine's Day present?" Mandy grinned.

Gran burst out laughing. "At least it won't wilt." She put the phone back in her pocket. "Seriously, Mandy, leave the matchmaking to others. If you want to be helpful, you could go to the post office for me and pick up something I ordered."

"What is it?"

"A new fishing hat for Grandad." She smiled sheepishly. "For Valentine's Day."

"Now that's what I call romantic." Mandy laughed.

Mandy was coming out of the post office half an hour later when she saw Mrs. Redman crossing the road toward her.

"Hi, Mrs. Redman."

"Hello, Mandy. I hear you're quite the heroine."

Mandy frowned.

"Condor," said Mrs. Redman. "Apparently you saved his life."

"I just carried him into Animal Ark," Mandy said. "It was Mom and Dad who saved him."

"You're too modest," said Mrs. Redman. "And I can tell you, Kate is over the moon."

"Is she Lord Fitzroy's girlfriend?" Mandy blurted out before she even realized what she was saying.

Mrs. Redman looked surprised. "His girlfriend? Goodness me, no. Kate's . . . well, let's just say she's not his type." She glanced around, as if to make sure no one was listening. "Lord Fitzroy doesn't even have a girlfriend. If you ask me"— she leaned forward and in a low voice said —"he never got over Carole."

It was exactly what Mandy wanted to hear. "You really think so?"

Mrs. Redman looked around again, then leaned in farther. "Apparently," she whispered, "Carole broke his heart."

"*She* broke *his* heart?" Mandy gasped.

"That's what the previous housekeeper, Mrs. Williams, told me," said Mrs. Redman.

"But it's not true," said Mandy. "Lord Fitzroy was the one who broke it off."

Two women were coming down the street toward them. Mrs. Redman took Mandy's arm and steered her back across the road to the bus stop. "What do you mean, 'he broke it off'?" she asked when they were sitting on the bench.

"Carole told me. She wrote to him at the university, but he never replied."

"That's not like him at all," said Mrs. Redman. "He must not have received the letters. And even if he wanted to break up with Carole, he'd have said so, rather than snubbing her. Lord Fitzroy always speaks his mind."

"He didn't this morning," Mandy said. "He came up with some silly excuses about why he needed to stop in at Carole's."

Mrs. Redman laughed so loudly that the women on the other side of the road turned around and stared at her. "He sounds like a lovestruck teenager," she said when the women went on their way again. "So I think," she added in her confidential tone, "we'll have to do something about it. Get them back together somehow."

"That's exactly what I was thinking," Mandy said.

Mrs. Redman took a package of jelly beans out of her bag. "Any ideas?" she asked, offering Mandy the candy.

Mandy chose a green one. "We'll have to think of an excuse to get Carole to Fitzroy Manor again. And for her and Lord Fitzroy to be left alone together."

"Mmm," said Mrs. Redman, popping a pink jelly bean into her mouth. "We could pretend I need to speak to her urgently about the cake stands."

"Sounds good," Mandy said just as another idea came to her. "And if Condor's better tomorrow, I could tell Carole I'm taking him to Fitzroy Manor. I could ask her to give us a ride."

"And I could line Lord Fitzroy up for an appointment with another guest," said Mrs. Redman. "The guest being Carole, of course. Only he won't know that until he sees her."

"It's going to be perfect!" Mandy declared, grinning at her coconspirator.

But on the way back to Animal Ark, she crossed her fingers. For it to work out, Condor had to be well enough to go home the next day.

At home, Mandy phoned James to tell him the plan. "It means we'll need all the diabetes information by tomorrow," she told him.

"I've printed out stacks of stuff," said James. "I'll bring it over today. Dad and I are going to a computer show in York tomorrow."

"That sounds right up your alley," Mandy said. James was very into computers and liked to keep up with the latest developments.

"Normally it would be," he said. "But I think I'd rather see Condor being reunited with his owner."

"I don't think even I'll see that," Mandy said. "It's just

Kate who'll be there tomorrow. The owner's coming the next day."

After she hung up, Mandy went to see Condor. She paused at the door, nervous to go in. What if he'd had a relapse? She took a deep breath and pushed open the door.

"Condor!" she gasped.

The corgi was on his feet! Standing straight and proud, his head held high, and with a regal expression on his intelligent face, he looked every inch a little prince.

"Hey! Look at you." Mandy laughed, going over to him. "So you *did* live up to your nickname."

He barked at her.

"What's all the noise?" said Simon, coming in just then.

"Look at Condor," Mandy said.

"Yeah, he rallied about half an hour ago. I've just been looking for you to tell you," said Simon.

"So suddenly?" Mandy exclaimed. "I mean, just yesterday it looked like he'd never wake up."

"That's the thing about diabetes," said Simon. "Once the blood sugar has been stabilized, and if there is no organ damage, the patient recovers really fast. Your mom and dad think Condor might even be able to go home in a day or two."

"Perfect!" Mandy said.

She stayed with Condor until James arrived. In that time, Dr. Emily came through with a special meal for the corgi. He ate it hungrily and when he'd finished, looked around for more.

"That's enough for now," said Dr. Emily. "And we're going to have to make sure you eat only the right things in the future." She took a piece of paper out of her pocket and showed it to Mandy. "We'll give his owner a copy of this."

It was a list of foods that Condor was not allowed to eat — things like very fatty foods and sugary treats which dogs shouldn't eat, anyway — and some brands of special prescription diets the owners could buy from their vet. There were also suggestions for a homemade diet if the owners didn't want to buy commercially prepared meals. For treats, Condor would be allowed to have rawhide bones or special low-calorie dog biscuits.

"Definitely no cupcake treats ever again," Mandy said.

James arrived armed with a wad of documents. "We might have to put it in a better order," he said after they'd left Condor sleeping soundly, content after his first good meal since his brush with death. "At the moment, it's a little messy."

They sat at the dining room table with the documents spread out in front of them. "We'll group them under different headings," Mandy said, "like symptoms, first aid, insulin treatment, and diet."

"What about recipes?" said James. "I found lots of them on the Internet."

"Great," Mandy said. "The more information the better."

It was early evening when they'd completed the project and the documents were organized in a neat-looking black folder. James had even printed out his photograph of Condor. He pasted it in the middle of the front cover with CONDOR written beneath it in large gold letters. There were other pictures, too, that he'd found on the Internet: pictures of dogs having blood taken, others of the different types of insulin available, and some of the different glucose monitors that people could buy along with the information about each one.

Dr. Adam was very impressed when he saw the finished product. "We should think about giving all our diabetic patients one of these," he said.

"It's easy enough," said James. "I'll make copies of everything. It's just the picture that will have to change every time."

With phase one of the "Valentine Reunion" plan complete, Mandy could hardly wait for phase two. The next morning, she called Carole and said she'd bumped into Mrs. Redman. "She'd like you to go over there this afternoon to make the final arrangements."

"I thought we'd done that," said Carole.

Mandy panicked for a moment, wondering if Carole would refuse to go.

"She's a bit frantic, I think," Mandy said, trying to think of ways to persuade Carole to go. "There was something about the cake stands, and how to arrange the cupcakes. I think she's nervous because of the VIP guest of honor." She felt bad that she wasn't telling the truth. *But it's for Carole's own good*, she told herself.

"Oh, all right," said Carole. "I'll take all the cupcakes, too, so that I don't have to go back there again on Valentine's Day."

Yes! Mandy said to herself in silent triumph. Carole didn't suspect a thing! "Oh, and if it's all right with you, I might be taking Condor up there, so maybe you would give us a ride?" she said, trying to sound casual.

"Sure," said Carole. "Is he completely better?"

"Close," Mandy said.

The morning dragged as slowly as if Mandy was sitting in a very boring class at school. Every time she looked at her watch, the hands had hardly moved. She kept checking on Condor, and each time she saw him, he seemed stronger. And he always greeted her with an excited bark and a wag of his tail. An hour before Carole was to arrive, Mandy's mom suggested they walk him in the yard to be doubly sure he was on the mend.

The corgi seemed delighted to find himself out in the open again. He scampered around the yard, his nose working overtime to identify the interesting smells he came across. His eyesight seemed just as sharp. Leaves scudding across the lawn in the wind, a blade of grass swaying, Mandy's feet — nothing that moved escaped his attention. He checked them all out, even nipping Mandy's heels so that she had to stand still.

A crow landed on the bird feeder to claim a chunk of suet Mandy's dad had put out earlier. Condor raced across the lawn toward it, barking with excitement, and ran after it as it flew away, like he was driving it out of the yard.

"His herding instinct's still there," Mandy said, chuckling.

"Indeed. And he's as fit as a fiddle," Dr. Emily laughed.

At two-thirty, Carole's pink van drove in through the gates. Fifteen minutes later, it drove out again, with Mandy and Condor sitting in the front with Carole. Mandy was secretly delighted to see how pretty Carole looked in a light pink sweater and brown jeans.

In the back of the van were stacks of cupcake boxes, the lids taped down to corgi-proof them. Also in the back was a shopping bag. It contained the information folder and all of Condor's medication. The vials of insulin were in a small styrofoam box that would have to go into the fridge at Fitzroy Manor. There was a pack of new syringes, too, a glucose test kit, and a letter from Mandy's parents to Condor's vet detailing the treatment he'd had at Animal Ark.

"Mom says we've covered everything, but we must be sure Condor's owners understand exactly what to do," Mandy said. The corgi was on her lap, watching the passing countryside through the window. He barked whenever he saw a horse or a cow in a field.

At Fitzroy Manor, Mrs. Redman met them in the courtyard. "I'll send someone to unpack the cupcakes," she said. She bent down and patted the corgi who greeted her with a woof and a wag of his little tail. "We don't want you getting into the cupcakes again, so we'll take you up to Kate at once."

She led Mandy, Carole, and Condor upstairs to a room at the end of another long passage. She knocked on the door. "Lady Katherine. Condor's arrived."

Lady Katherine! Mandy gulped. She'd imagined Kate would be an ordinary person, like her and Carole.

"Excellent! Do come in." The voice was very regal.

Out of the corner of her eye, Mandy saw Carole stiffen. At her feet, Condor pricked up his ears and barked. He must have recognized the voice.

Mrs. Redman opened the door. "In you go, Condor,"

she said as he scampered past her. "If you'll excuse me," she said to Mandy and Carole, "I'll make sure the cupcakes have been brought in. When you're ready, come to the kitchen and we'll see to the . . . um . . . other arrangements." She brushed past Mandy, nudging her arm. "See you shortly."

Inside the room, a woman was bending down to pat Condor who bounced around her, licking her face, and making high-pitched excited noises.

"Silly boy," said Lady Katherine. "Slipping out of your collar and running off like that. I thought we'd lost you for good."

Mandy wanted to say, *You nearly did*, but that would sound rude so she kept silent. She waited for a chance to hand over the information pack and medication. Carole was standing just inside the door next to Mandy, watching the happy reunion, but looking impatient.

At last, Lady Katherine stood up and looked across the room to Mandy and Carole.

She's exactly like her voice, was Mandy's first thought. *Very elegant!*

Lady Katherine was probably a few years older than Carole. Her black hair was short and neat, and she wore a tailored navy skirt and matching jacket that would have been immaculate earlier but now sported lots of light-tan corgi hairs. She smiled at Mandy and Carole. "I don't know how to thank you."

"I can't take any credit," said Carole. "It was Mandy who found Condor."

"I'm really very grateful to you, Mandy," said Lady Katherine. "If he hadn't been found, his owner would have been heartbroken."

"It's lucky we found him in time," Mandy said, watching him jump easily onto a sofa. "And that Mom and Dad could treat him."

Kate looked over her shoulder to where Condor was stretched out on the sofa, his head on a silk cushion. "I know you've been sick, Condor, but that is taking liberties," she said. She pointed to a wicker basket next to the sofa. It stood on little stilts a few inches off the ground and had a tartan blanket inside. "There's your bed."

The corgi obediently jumped down and climbed into the basket.

"Good boy," said Kate. "And as agile as ever." She smiled at Mandy and Kate. "He seems none the worse for his illness."

"Luckily not. But diabetes is very serious," Mandy said; she was worried the situation might be played down now that Condor looked so healthy. She held out the carrier bag. "There's an information pack in here along with his medication."

Lady Katherine smiled and took it from her. "Thank you, Mandy. I'm sure this will be very helpful."

"You *will* give it to his owners, won't you?" Mandy prompted. "So they can find out exactly how to handle Condor's illness."

"Owner," Lady Katherine corrected Mandy with a smile. She put the bag on an antique bureau next to her. "And I promise you, she will do everything and more to ensure that Condor stays in the best of health."

"She'll have to watch him very closely," Mandy went on. "I know he looks great now, so it'll probably be hard for her to understand just how bad he was."

Lady Katherine smiled again. "I wouldn't worry too much about that."

"No, it's important," Mandy insisted. "Maybe Mom and Dad should speak to her. Or I could."

"Mandy knows a lot about handling him," said Carole. "She even stayed up for a whole night to make sure he was OK. Condor's owner could learn a lot from her."

"I'm sure she'd love to talk to you, Mandy, but she's very busy," said Lady Katherine. "She'll be at the banquet tomorrow, but she won't have a moment to meet you."

Mandy must have looked upset because Lady Katherine quickly added, "Please don't take that as an insult."

"I'm not insulted," Mandy said. "I'm just wondering how anyone could be too busy to discuss a precious pet who is so sick."

Lady Katherine didn't answer. She looked away and drummed her fingers on the antique bureau.

Puzzled, Mandy traded a look with Carole. *What did I say?*

"We need to be discreet about visits," Lady Katherine suddenly said, looking at Mandy again. "It's about security, you see."

Mandy didn't see at all. *What is she worried about?*

"I think you should know," said Lady Katherine. "Condor belongs to the queen."

Nine

"The queen!" Mandy could hardly believe her ears.

"Condor is Her Majesty's favorite dog," said Kate. "When she heard he was missing, she nearly sent her troops out to find him! And then we learned that you'd not only found him, but saved his life."

Mandy wanted to say it was her parents who saved him, but no words came out when she tried to speak. At the same time, it was hard to believe that a dog belonging to the queen of England could have been so sick with no one knowing. And then she remembered that Type 1 diabetes could develop very fast without any warning.

"Her Majesty is devastated that he's diabetic," Kate said as if she guessed what was going through Mandy's mind. "There was no sign of anything being amiss. Until, of course, you found him after he'd gorged himself on cupcakes."

"I'm so sorry about that!" Carole gasped, and Mandy saw her turn pale. "It's my fault."

Kate frowned. "Your fault?"

"Yes. I made the cupcakes."

"*You're* Carole?" Kate asked, and Mandy couldn't decide whether she looked surprised, angry, or impressed. "I've heard a lot about you."

"Really?" said Carole. She sounded touchy. She probably still thought that Kate was Edward's girlfriend. "Look," Carole went on, "if I could have predicted that Condor would climb into the van and . . ."

Kate shook her head and raised both hands. "No, you misunderstand me. You're not to blame. Condor's a terrible glutton, like many corgis are. We have to be very careful that he doesn't put on too much weight. And I can tell you something else." She lowered her voice, like she was about to share a secret. "You're not the only one who blamed herself, Carole. I blamed myself for him disappearing, and the queen felt terrible that her beloved dog was sick without her picking up on it."

"She shouldn't feel guilty for a minute," Mandy said, finding her voice again. "Type One diabetes isn't easy to spot until there's a crisis."

"That just *might* help Her Majesty feel better," said Kate. She tapped the folder. "And I know she'll appreciate this a lot. You've done a great job, Mandy."

"It wasn't just me," she said. "My best friend, James Hunter, helped a lot, too. And my mom and dad, of course."

Their excited voices must have woken Condor. He sat up in his basket, looking around like someone expecting to be waited on. Mandy went to pat him. She felt as if she were in a dream. *Who'd have thought we'd saved the queen's corgi?* She stroked the white crown-shaped patch on his neck. He straightened his back and lifted his chin, looking more regal than ever.

"I was right all along," Mandy chuckled. "You *are* a little prince!"

With Kate and Condor happily back together, it was time for the next big reunion.

"We're ready to get back to the arrangements," Mandy said, giving Mrs. Redman a secret wink when she and Carole returned to the kitchen.

"Good, good," said the housekeeper. "Let me see . . ." She glanced at the boxes of cupcakes on the counters.

She seemed flustered again, but Mandy knew that this time it was just an act to stop Carole from suspecting anything. "We need to take those," she said, pointing to three ornate cake stands on the table, "into the dining room."

"OK," said Carole, picking one up. "Lead the way."

Mrs. Redman waited for Carole's back to be turned, then she gave Mandy a double thumbs-up. *So far, so good*, she implied.

In the dining room, Mrs. Redman didn't even pause, but led them straight past the huge table and through a door at the far side.

They entered a gorgeous room — a glass conservatory that made Mandy feel as if she'd arrived in a tropical forest. She was surrounded by plants, some with enormous glossy leaves, others that were dainty ferns cascading down from hanging baskets. There were orchids, too, exotic and beautiful, their heady perfume filling the air.

"This is incredible!" Mandy gasped, staring at the view beyond the French doors — the glistening lake where three swans glided like tall ships on a calm sea.

Carole, however, seemed confused. "Is this where the cakes are going to be served?" She frowned at the small round table in the middle of the room. It was covered with a starched white tablecloth. Two places were set with white bone-china cups and saucers and plates, linen napkins, and silver cutlery. And in the middle, in a silver vase, was a single long-stemmed red rose. "What's . . ." a look of dismay came over her, "going . . . on?" she said in slow motion as Edward entered through the French doors.

"Mrs. Briggs said you wanted to . . ." Edward broke off as he saw Carole standing next to a white orchid on the other side of the room. "See me," he murmured.

Mrs. Redman took control. "Sit down, both of you," she said, and Mandy smiled at her bossy tone.

"I've made tea for you," Mrs. Redman continued. "Mandy and I will bring it through in a minute." Before anyone could say another word, she took the cake stand from Carole and bustled out. "Come along, Mandy."

Mandy had just enough time to see Carole glaring at her before she hurried out, too.

In the kitchen, Mrs. Redman handed Mandy a black-and-white uniform. "You'll make a lovely waitress," she said, and showed her to the staff coatroom nearby.

When she'd changed, Mandy stared at the mirror. She hardly recognized herself. In the stiff, black, button-up dress, with its short sleeves, frilly white apron, and starched white cap, she looked like an old-fashioned maid.

"You suit the role perfectly," said Mrs. Redman when Mandy returned to the kitchen. "Except for those shoes."

Mandy looked down at her bulky blue sneakers. They did look out of place. A pair of sensible, neat black shoes, like the ones Jean Knox wore, would have been better.

"Never mind," said Mrs. Redman. "I'm sure our guests will be too wrapped up in each other to notice." She picked up a tray. On it was a silver teapot, a plate of dainty cucumber sandwiches arranged in a circle, and another plate with freshly baked cream scones, still warm from the oven. "Would you take this through to them, please?"

Passing through the dining room again, Mandy felt nervous. What if it all was a big mistake, and Carole and Edward didn't like each other after all? Carole had looked really angry, too, when she saw it was a setup. *Gran was right. Maybe it's not such a good idea to arrange other people's lives for them.*

It was done, though, and Mandy had to face the consequences. She paused at the conservatory door, took a deep breath, and pushed it open.

Her worst fears were confirmed.

"I know about Kate — or rather, Lady Katherine," Carole was saying. She sat sideways at the table, her arms crossed.

"What do you know?" said Edward. He was leaning forward, looking grim.

Carole didn't look at him but gazed out of the window at the lake. "That she's your . . . she's probably the one you, you know . . ." She looked at Edward. "The one you met at Cambridge."

"At Cambridge?" Edward sat up straight and folded his arms. "What are you talking about? Kate is Lady Katherine Anstey, the queen's lady-in-waiting. She's engaged to be married to Lord Peter Winslow in July."

"Oh," said Carole in a very small voice and blushed.

Oh, dear, Mandy thought, and wished the floor would swallow her up as both Carole and Edward turned to see her coming in.

But Edward only glanced at Mandy before leaning forward again. He put his elbows on the table and rested his chin on his hands. "What happened, Carole? To us?"

"Us?" She looked right into his eyes. "There was no us. You went away. I didn't." She stood up abruptly, gave Mandy another angry look, and said, "There's been a mistake. We must go."

"No!" Mandy said, slamming the tray down on the table a lot harder than she'd meant to. The neat circle of cucumber sandwiches collapsed like a set of dominoes. "Edward . . . Lord Fitzroy never got the letters."

"Letters?" said Edward.

"I wrote," said Carole. Mandy saw her swallow. "Every third day, for two weeks. You never replied."

"I never received them!" Edward stood up and went over to Carole. "I'm so sorry," he said, and put his hand on her arm.

Carole looked at his hand. "Well, it was a long time ago."

"It's like yesterday," said Edward. "Remember the day I left for Cambridge?"

Carole nodded.

"Beulah wouldn't start, and I said it was a sign I shouldn't go."

"You were always superstitious," said Carole, and Mandy saw a hint of a smile on her face.

Time to get out of here, she thought. She poured out the tea and put the plates of sandwiches and scones on the table. "Tea's ready," she said, and started to back away.

"Thank you," said Edward. "Ah, Earl Grey," he added, breathing in the steam rising from the cups. "Isn't that your favorite, Carole?"

She nodded and smiled as he pulled out her chair for her. She'd just sat down when there came a sound like galloping horses from the garden. Moments later, four sets of legs skidded to a stop at the French doors.

"The dogs!" Mandy laughed.

Horatio and Gilbert pawed at the door, begging to be let in. Behind them, Hobbit stood swinging his tail in a goofy way. And almost lost among the Great Danes' gangly lampstand-like legs was Condor, barking like he was calling out orders.

"We'll have to let them in or there'll be a riot." Edward laughed and went to the door.

It felt like a riot when the four charged in. Gilbert and Hobbit jostled Edward, each trying to get noticed first. Horatio raced to the table to greet Carole, and nearly wiped the cream scones onto the floor with his tail.

Mandy dove forward and grabbed the scones just in time. Condor was waiting right next to the table, ready to devour any food that came his way.

"Why don't I take you four to the kitchen?" Mandy said, clapping her hands to get their attention. She bent down and picked up Condor. "You can have a snack there, Your Highness. A nice plain doggy biscuit. With no butter, sugar, cream, or jam."

Condor licked his lips and barked. *Anything that you're serving*, he seemed to say.

Darkness was falling when Mandy and Carole drove away from Fitzroy Manor. Mandy had lost count of how many times she'd refreshed the teapot. And each time she took it back into the conservatory, Carole and Edward seemed happier and more relaxed in each other's company.

"I had a fabulous afternoon," Carole said, driving through the gate.

"I thought I'd made a big mistake," Mandy admitted. "Gran said I shouldn't interfere."

"I must admit I was annoyed to start with," said Carole. "And then came your little outburst about the letters."

"Sorry," Mandy said.

"Don't apologize," said Carole. "It was the best thing you could have done. Thanks to that, we were able to clear everything up. Edward's even invited me to the banquet tomorrow."

"Wow!" Mandy said. "You'll meet the queen."

Carole winced. "Oh, yes! I'd nearly forgotten." She smiled. "I'll have to find a fancy dress. And practice my curtsy!"

A flurry of snow drifted across their path. In the van's headlights, the delicate flakes sparkled like diamonds. "It looks so romantic," Mandy said.

"Pure magic," said Carole.

But as far as Mandy was concerned, the really magical thing was that she'd been looking after a royal corgi!

She couldn't wait to tell James everything. At home, she called him straightaway. "But don't tell anyone the queen's going to be at the banquet," she finished, remembering her promise to be discreet.

"That's awesome," said James. "I wish I'd been there when you found out who Condor belongs to. But the main thing is that he's better and he's back home."

"Almost back home," Mandy said, which was more than she could say for Nomad. In a way, she felt that she'd failed him. He'd been at Animal Ark for three days and she wasn't any closer to finding out where he'd come from, or why he was still in England in the winter. "I wonder," she said to James, "if we could search the Internet to find out more about honey buzzards."

"Sure. When do you want to come over?"

"Now, if that's OK. Dad's going to a meeting in Walton. He can give me a ride."

When Mandy arrived at James's house, he was already at the computer, researching honey buzzards. "This is the best site so far," he said. "I've even heard the sound that honey buzzards make."

It was the Web site for the Royal Society for the Protection of Birds. Mandy pulled up a chair and started reading. "It says there aren't many honey buzzards in the UK," she said as James scrolled down the page. "And they're mainly in the south and east, and in northern Scotland from about May to September. That's when they fly south again to Africa."

"And look at this," said James. "Their nest sites have to be kept secret so that egg collectors don't raid them."

"Imagine stealing a rare bird's eggs!" Mandy said hotly. "In fact, stealing any bird's eggs is cruel."

"Hen's eggs, too?" said James with a teasing smile.

"You know what I mean," said Mandy.

James pointed to the screen. "Listen to this. 'Honey buzzards are found only in woodlands and upland conifer forests.'" He looked at Mandy. "That probably explains why they aren't found in Yorkshire. It's not exactly the most forested county in England."

The Web site gave details of the route the birds followed when they migrated to Africa in autumn. They flew over the south and east coasts, hardly ever straying inland. "So it looks like Yorkshire is just about the last place anyone could expect to find them," Mandy said. "Even in summer."

"So what is Nomad doing in Welford in winter?" said James.

Mandy sighed. "That's the million-dollar question."

Nothing on the Web site had even hinted at an answer. "We're back to square one. All I can think is that he must have gotten lost."

Later, back at Animal Ark, Mandy went to see Nomad before she went to bed. She found her mom with him, looking worried.

"What's the matter?" Mandy asked.

"I don't like the look of him," said Dr. Emily. "He should have perked up by now, but he's not eating, he's obviously in some discomfort, and he's lethargic."

There could be no doubt about that. Nomad was hunched up on the floor of the cage, his eyes half-closed, and his head drooping.

"I'm having to treat those wounds again," said Dr. Emily. "I thought they were from the collision with the truck, but I've had a chance to look at them more closely and it seems that he already had most of them from some earlier accident. I even found some others beneath his wings. Some have already healed, but some are definitely infected and there's a bit of necrosis around one or two of them."

"Necrosis?" Mandy echoed.

"It's when some of the tissue dies because the blood supply to it was interrupted. I just hope we're not too late to do something about these bigger wounds." She put on a pair of gloves, then reached into the cage and brought Nomad out. "You hold his wrists so that he doesn't struggle."

Remembering how her mom had held Nomad on that first day, Mandy stood behind him and gripped the bones of his wrists. His wings didn't even twitch. Mandy felt her heart sink. "It's like he's given up," she said. "But why now? How could he have kept going so long with all those wounds?"

Dr. Emily was dabbing the worst of the cuts with swabs soaked in iodine. "Even big birds like Nomad are vulnerable to larger predators," she explained. "Especially when they're weak or injured. To escape being seen as easy prey, birds will often try to hide injuries or illnesses."

"You mean, they behave normally? They keep going no matter what?" Mandy asked.

"That about sums it up," said Dr. Emily.

"Then that explains it all," Mandy said, putting two and two together.

"What?" Her mom frowned.

"Why Nomad ended up in Yorkshire."

Her mom shook her head. "Sorry, you've lost me, Mandy."

"Think about it," Mandy said, watching her mom squeeze some sterile lubricant from a tube onto some of Nomad's wounds. "Whatever caused all those cuts in the first place made Nomad so weak he couldn't manage the migration journey. So he got left behind, perhaps in Scotland, when all the other honey buzzards flew south at the end of summer."

"But that doesn't explain why he's in Yorkshire," said Dr. Emily.

"It does," Mandy said. "As winter set in, he found less and less to eat, which made him grow weaker and weaker." The picture of the honey buzzard desperately looking for food in the bleak winter landscape was almost more than she could bear. "Then those strong winds started. Remember how all those branches blew down last week?"

Dr. Emily nodded.

Mandy continued. "He was too weak to battle the winds and they blew him here, way off course. Eventually, he couldn't fly anymore and that's when he crash-landed into the truck."

Her mom looked thoughtful. "You might have a point. It does make sense."

As she eased Nomad back into the cage, Mandy stroked the silky feathers on his wings. "You poor brave boy," she said, her heart going out to him even more.

Not only was he hurt and alone, he was probably the only honey buzzard in Britain.

Ten

Nomad's situation looked bleaker than ever.

"All we can do is wait and hope the infections clear up before we can even think about what to do with him," said Dr. Emily.

For Mandy, that wasn't enough. "We've got to help him build up his strength. He *must* eat."

"I agree, sweetie. He must be lacking nutrients he'd get from his normal diet," said Dr. Emily. "We've tried bits of chicken and meat, but he's rejected that."

Mandy remembered what the RSPB Web site had said about honey buzzards' diets. "They eat mainly wasps and bees and their larvae."

"Not many of those around this time of the year," said her mom.

"They eat worms, too," Mandy remembered. "We'll just have to dig up some earthworms."

Early the next morning, Mandy and James were kneeling in the flowerbeds at Animal Ark, digging up the muddy earth.

"There's one!" Mandy said as her trowel unearthed a long, pinkish-brown worm. "Yuck!" she said, picking it up and putting it in a jar.

"Not nearly as yucky as watching our moms and dads give each other sappy Valentines," said James, finding another worm and popping it into the jar.

Mandy punched him playfully on his arm. "Valentines aren't that bad." She thought of Carole and how she must be so excited about the banquet. "For some people, it means a lot."

"These poor worms aren't in for a romantic Valentine's Day," said James, digging up another one. "Being a honey buzzard's breakfast can't exactly be pleasant. It's a bit cruel, what we're doing."

Mandy wrinkled her nose. "It is sort of gruesome. But I suppose it's part of the natural order. We're not really interfering with nature by finding food for a sick raptor."

"And if you were one of these worms? Would you say that?" said James.

"Stop it, James! Sometimes we just have to accept that there are predators and there is prey." Mandy wiped a strand of hair out of her eyes with the back of her hand. As she did, she looked up and glimpsed a large shape skim across the sky above the roof of the house. She caught her breath. "Did you see that?"

"What?"

"That bird. It was big. Like Nomad." Mandy jumped up in the hope she'd catch another glimpse of it. But it had disappeared.

"You're imagining things," said James, scanning the sky, too.

"I'm not," Mandy said. "I definitely saw something. What if it *was* a honey buzzard?"

James flicked an earthworm off his trowel into the jar. "Impossible. And you know it. Your mind's working overtime from all your schemes to get Carole and Lord Fitzroy back together. If it *was* a bird, it was probably a raven."

They took the earthworms in to Nomad, putting them in a dish inside the cage. Nomad didn't even open his eyes so Mandy and James left him, hoping he'd begin his meal as soon as he woke up.

"I hope the worms don't slither away," said James.

They went to wash their hands in the kitchen and to make some hot chocolate to warm themselves up. Mandy was filling up the kettle at the sink when, through the window, she saw a truck coming down the lane. It pulled over and stopped just outside the gate. "It's the truck that Nomad flew into," Mandy said. "The driver must have come to get his sweater."

They went outside to meet him.

"How's the bird?" he asked as soon as he saw them.

"Not too good," Mandy said. "Would you like to see him, Mr., um . . . ?"

"Call me Alexander," said the driver. "And yes, that's why I'm here. To see him."

"And to get your sweater," Mandy said.

"Oh, yes," said Alexander. "I'd nearly forgotten about that."

Going inside, Mandy and James told Alexander everything they knew about Nomad. "One of the worst things is that he's completely alone," Mandy said.

"And he doesn't even want to try to eat," said James. "It's like he's finally given up."

But when they went into the wildlife unit they saw that, far from giving up, Nomad was growing restless. He was wide awake now and flapping his wings, beating them against the wire. The cage was too small for him to stretch them out fully.

"Be careful, Nomad," Mandy said. "You'll hurt yourself." She winced as he battered his wings against the bars.

"The worms are gone," James said. "He must have eaten them."

"That's probably why he's feeling more energetic," said Alexander.

It was a tricky situation. It was great to see Nomad regaining strength but now he ran the risk of hurting himself more. "I'll get Mom or Dad," Mandy said, going out to call them.

Dr. Adam had a few minutes between patients, so he came to check on Nomad. "He's not doing himself any good, flapping his wings like that," he said. "I'll sedate him and we'll have to come up with a plan fast. We can't let him go, and we can't keep him in that cage."

"Would a smaller cage help?" asked Alexander. "So he couldn't flap his wings at all?"

Dr. Adam injected the sedative into Nomad. "A bigger cage would be better, actually, so that he can spread his wings. A small one *would* stop him from flapping but it could also crush his tail and wings and he wouldn't be able to fly correctly when we let him go."

"We don't have a big enough cage," Mandy said.

"I think I can help," said Alexander. "Come and see."

They went out to his truck. "There are stacks of fencing in here that's going to a scrap yard," he said, opening the back doors and pulling himself up. "I could use some of it to make an aviary for Nomad." He disappeared for a moment and reappeared holding a huge piece of wire mesh. "What do you think?"

"That we should get started now," Mandy said.

Dr. Adam had to return to his patients, but Mandy and James helped Alexander to unload enough wire mesh to construct the aviary. They took it to the backyard, and for the next hour, worked fast joining the panels with wire ties. At last, the aviary was ready. It was about ten feet tall, eight feet wide, and twenty feet long, with a gate at one end. James rigged up a perch in one corner, made from a branch that had blown down in the wind, and Mandy found a wooden crate that could serve as a snug shelter. She put dry grass and sticks inside it, hoping it was something like a honey buzzard's nest.

"It's not exactly Buckingham Palace," said Alexander, standing back to look at the finished product. "But it's sturdy, and big enough for a honey buzzard."

When Mandy's parents saw it, they gave it their approval. "It'll give him a chance to exercise his wings," said Dr. Emily. "So when he is strong enough, he'll be able to fly."

"And then what?" asked James.

Neither Dr. Adam or Dr. Emily could answer the question. "It's a tough one," said Mandy's dad. "We can't just let him go at this stage. He's unlikely to join up with other honey buzzards since he's so far from their normal migration route."

"What about the RSPB?" asked Alexander. "Couldn't they take him and release him in the summer where there are other honey buzzards?"

It seemed to be the best solution to Mandy, until James asked if the other buzzards would be willing to accept Nomad.

"They might not," said Dr. Adam. "Especially during the breeding season. Breeding pairs might be very territorial and would drive off other birds."

"And Nomad would be just that," Mandy said. "A nomad, and a very lonely one."

With Nomad's prospects looking so grim, Mandy felt very gloomy. She spent the day helping around Animal Ark and watching Nomad in his new home. She hoped he'd start flying as soon as he was in the aviary. But he sat at one end of the cage, only ruffling his feathers every now and then. It was as if he knew that he faced an uncertain future.

Downhearted, Mandy finally left Nomad when it grew dark. She cheered up a bit when the pink van pulled up in the driveway an hour later.

"I thought I'd stop by on my way to the banquet," said Carole when Mandy opened the front door.

Mandy stared at her, impressed. Carole looked amazing! Her hair was piled up in soft curls and held in place by a sparkling barrette. She wore a pair of diamond earrings that caught the light and turned it into glittering, dancing rays. Her long blue dress seemed to have been designed for her alone; it fit her like a glove and was made of shimmering silk that whispered when she moved. Even her shoes were dazzling; elegant, high-heeled silver sandals that complemented the diamond earrings.

"You look lovely!" Mandy managed to say at last.

"Thank you," said Carole, smiling. She touched the tiara and earrings. "Aren't these gorgeous?"

"Are they real diamonds?" Mandy asked.

Carole nodded. "Can you believe it? Carole, the girl from Welford, the local home-baker, in real diamonds!"

"And why not?" Mandy challenged. "I can't imagine anyone looking more lovely in them than you do."

Carole's cheeks blushed. "That's what Edward said when he gave them to me this morning."

"A Valentine's gift!" Mandy said, completely satisfied — and very impressed with Lord Fitzroy's generosity and good taste. Things had worked out even better than she'd hoped.

"I've brought you all a gift, too," Carole said, and Mandy noticed a box she'd brought in and put on the hall table. "To thank you for all your help."

Inside the box were a dozen cupcakes. Instead of a dainty rose on top, they were each decorated with a different animal. There was a black stallion like the statue at Fitzroy Manor, two Great Danes, two kittens that were identical to Meg and Mog, two Labradors, one black, the other yellow, a bird that might have been Nomad, three swans like the ones on the lake at the manor, and, best of all, a caramel-colored corgi with white markings. "He looks exactly like Condor!" Mandy exclaimed.

When her dad saw the cupcakes, he reached for the black Labrador. "Not that one!" Mandy said, tapping his hand. "That looks like Blackie, so we should save it for James."

Two days later, Mandy went out after breakfast to take more earthworms to Nomad. He had been eating well since his first meal, but so far had shown little interest in his new surroundings. So when Mandy approached the aviary, and he swooped from his perch to the wooden shelter at the other end, she was over the moon. "You look magnificent!" she said, seeing his broad wings stretched out full.

There was more good news. When Dr. Emily examined the wounds later that morning, she pronounced that they were healing well. "I think we've got the infection under control. So with that, and him being able to exercise his wings, he should be fit to fly again very soon."

But fly where? Mandy wondered. She pictured other honey buzzards soaring above the distant African bushland. In just a few short months, in late April, they'd set out in huge numbers, winging their way back north again, over the Mediterranean Sea and Gibraltar, and over the Black Sea, too, and continuing to their breeding grounds in Europe and England and Scotland. Would Nomad ever be able to join them?

"Mandy! Emily!" Jean Knox's voice, urgent and excited, cut into Mandy's thoughts.

"We'd better go and see what happened," said Dr. Emily.

Jean was standing in the middle of the waiting room, clutching a letter, her eyes wide. Clustered around her were three other people with their pets: a Chihuahua, a Persian kitten, and an elderly poodle.

"This arrived for you just now, Mandy. Special delivery, too," said Jean, breathless with excitement. She handed her the letter. "Will you just look at where it came from?"

The envelope, thick and white, was addressed to Mandy. She turned it over and saw that it bore a scarlet seal in the shape of a crown. "The royal seal," she gasped. "It's from the palace!"

"The palace!" echoed the kitten's owner, a tiny woman who stood next to Mandy on tiptoes so she could see the seal for herself.

Mandy opened the envelope and took out the letter. It was handwritten, and signed by Lady Katherine.

"*Her Majesty wishes to extend her personal gratitude to you and your family for saving Condor,*'" Mandy read aloud.

"The queen!" The kitten's owner gasped.

"*He is in perfect health once more, chasing the pigeons in the palace gardens, sneaking onto Her Majesty's bed when no one is looking, and nipping the heels of unsuspecting footmen as if he feels obliged to herd them.*' I know just how that feels." Mandy chuckled. "*The queen is also very grateful for the information you and James prepared for her. She has read through everything in the folder, and she keeps it close at hand even when, like now, she's taking a short holiday in the country with her dogs. She administers Condor's insulin herself, and supervises his meals closely. Her Majesty thought you might enjoy the enclosed photograph.*'" Mandy held up the picture for everyone to see. It was of Condor sitting up very straight on a purple velvet cushion.

"My, what a regal little fellow," said the Chihuahua's owner. "He's quite the little prince."

Mandy smiled. "That's what I said from the very start."

Eleven

"All good things come to an end," Mandy said. It was Saturday, two days later. The school secretary had just called to say the boiler was fixed and classes would resume on Monday morning.

"I'd better get out my science book again," Mandy said.

"That would be a waste of our last two days of freedom," said James. "There are tons more exciting things to do than study for a test." He dropped a wriggling earthworm into a jar.

But Mandy was hardly listening to him. She'd heard

something else; a distant, high-pitched sound. "Listen!" she said, standing up.

"To what?"

"That sound. Like a bird's call," Mandy said, looking up at the sky. "It reminds me of . . . of . . ." She tried to place it, then suddenly thought she had. "Do you remember the honey buzzard's call we heard on the RSPB Web site?"

James stood up. "Something like this? *Peee-lu.*"

High above them, like an echo, came the distant sound again. *Peee-lu.*

"That's it!" Mandy gasped. "Wait there." She charged inside, grabbed a pair of binoculars, and was back in a flash, scanning the sky for the bird that she knew had to be a honey buzzard.

"Can you see it?" James prompted.

"No," Mandy said, frustrated.

"Maybe it's Nomad," suggested James as Mandy lowered the binoculars.

"It can't be," Mandy said. "The call was too distant, he's just a few yards away in the backyard." But as she said this, a shiver ran down her spine. "What if he's escaped?"

They dashed around to the backyard. When Mandy saw Nomad on his perch inside the aviary, she felt faint with relief. She couldn't bear the thought of him alone and at the mercy of the harsh winter yet again, when he'd only just started getting stronger. But where had the call come from? "Was that you calling?" she asked.

Nomad responded with a restless flapping of his wings. He put his head on one side and then the other, as if he too had heard something and was trying to figure it out.

The call came again, this time from somewhere beyond the aviary. *Peee-lu.* Louder now and clearer.

Then to her amazement, Mandy saw Nomad open his beak and reply: *Peee-lu.*

It was a heart-stopping moment. "You're answering, Nomad," she whispered.

"It's *got* to be another honey buzzard," said James, trying to locate it in the sky.

Nomad flapped his mighty wings again and looked up at the sky, too.

"Can you see it, Nomad?" Mandy asked, raising her binoculars. At first, she saw nothing but gray clouds. But just as she was about to lower the binoculars, a shape glided into sight. It was dark, with broad wings and a long, barred tail. "It *is* a honey buzzard," she whispered. "Nomad's not the only one in England after all." She gave the binoculars to James.

"It must be the one you saw on Valentine's Day," he said, watching it circling above them.

As Mandy held the bird in sight, she saw it angle its wings so that they were close to its sides. In the blink of an eye, it plunged down from the sky and swooped past the aviary, calling, *Peee-lu.*

Peee-lu, Nomad whistled back and, spreading his wings, he dove from his perch and glided the length of the aviary, parallel with the free-flying bird.

"It's like they know each other," said James.

"He does have a friend after all," Mandy said, tears in her eyes.

Nomad flew back and forth, calling out to the other bird as it swooped past him again, then with a powerful downstroke of its wings, soared up to the roof and landed on the wire.

There was only one thing to do. "Keep an eye on them, James," Mandy said, racing inside to get her parents.

When they returned, they saw the second honey buzzard standing on the roof of Nomad's aviary. Inside, Nomad was flying around, calling out in a near frenzy of excitement.

"His friend's come back for him," Mandy explained.

"Incredible!" Dr. Emily managed to say.

"Perhaps it never migrated," said James. "And it's been looking for Nomad all along."

Dr. Adam was shaking his head in amazement. "I'd never have believed it possible," he said. "The bird's a female by the way — her eyes are yellow — so she's probably Nomad's mate."

"We've got to let him go," Mandy said as the female suddenly took off, and Nomad flew across the aviary, looking frantic.

Mandy's parents looked at each other.

"He seems strong and he's flying well," said Dr. Adam. "But let's make sure those wounds are all right."

They opened the gate just wide enough to slip inside, but Nomad wouldn't let the Hopes near him. He dove off his perch and flew to the far side of the cage, landing on the wooden shelter Mandy had given him.

Dr. Emily watched him. "Well, we can keep him here a few days longer to make sure he's better," she said, "and watch him go crazy trying to join up with the female. Or we could let him go and hope that he's well enough to fend for himself."

"Let him go!" Mandy and James chorused together.

"He's not as vulnerable now," Mandy added. "And he has a companion to watch over him."

"We've done everything humans could do for him," said Dr. Emily. "It's time for nature to take over. "

"Let's do it, then," said Dr. Adam.

Mandy's mom and dad came out of the aviary, leaving the gate wide open.

"You're free, Nomad," Mandy whispered, watching the buzzard through the wire mesh.

Nomad met her gaze for a moment and blinked his bright orange eyes. Then he spread his wings and lifted effortlessly off the perch, swooping through the open door and soaring up out of the garden. His mate glided down to meet him, and their wings almost touched as they swirled above the roof of Animal Ark. A high-pitched *Peee-lu* rang out as the pair circled the yard, soaring higher and higher in perfect symmetry, reunited at last.

Mandy felt tears streaming down her cheeks. It was an incredible, miraculous reunion, and as romantic as Carole and Edward's.

"A wonderful ending to an amazing story," said Dr. Emily, turning to go back to her patients. But she stopped when one of the birds suddenly angled its wings and doubled back. It circled Animal Ark once before swooping low past Mandy and the others, turning his head at exactly the right moment, so that Mandy saw the orange of his eyes.

"Good-bye, Nomad!" she called to him as he soared into the sky again.

Peee-lu, he called out once more, and Mandy knew in her heart that he'd come back to say, "Thank you."

As the pair came together again and flew away from Animal Ark, Mandy, her mom and dad, and James ran to the fence to catch a last glimpse of them flying freely into their future. Through her binoculars Mandy watched them grow smaller and smaller until they were just specks on the horizon.

"Good luck," she called as they vanished at last. She was about to lower the binoculars when something else caught her attention. It was a dark-green object moving across the distant field. She adjusted the glasses to focus on it and saw that it was a Land Rover. It stopped at the top of a hill. A man climbed out from the passenger's side, and a woman from the driver's seat. She wore a head scarf, a green raincoat, and a pair of green waterproof boots. She held the door open and a dog jumped out.

A stocky, long-bodied, caramel-colored dog.

A corgi! And one that Mandy would recognize anywhere.

"Condor," she whispered as she watched the energetic dog race across the field, his royal owner walking briskly after him. "The corgi in the cupcakes!"